Wolf's Point

Book One of "River Detective"

by

Michael Robertson

Contents

Other Books by Michael Robertson

Butterfly Woman – Collected Short Stories (2007)

Natural Boy – Novella (2008)

The Lazlo Mission – Novel (2015)

CHAPTER ONE

Death in the Countryside

MARTIN CONRAD WAS CONFUSED by his new powers. He hadn't meant to kill the Amish man. And earlier that day, at the library, he hadn't meant to hurt the guy who wanted to hit him. He just needed gas for his truck and a way to get warm again. But sometimes magic takes you by surprise.

MARTIN RAN OUT OF GAS somewhere between Prairie Home and Jamestown on his way home to Wolf's Point. There was nothing around him on the lonely blacktop but farms. It was fall and the sun was down. The twilight that remained gave no heat and Martin hadn't thought to bring a coat. He stood next to the old Ford pickup his father had handed off to him a few weeks ago when he turned sixteen. It was a field truck without plates, meaning Martin could get arrested for driving on the highway.

Martin walked south, toward the river and home, until he found a driveway leading to a farmhouse set a long way off the road. He could see the white of a house and a barn lit by a dim light mounted high on a pole. He didn't know what else to do, so he started walking toward the barn. Maybe he would find some gas he could carry back to the truck.

Benedict Petersheim picked up the long pole with the hook on the end that stood tilted by the side door of his parent's house. Now his house, he reminded himself. His and his sister Felicity. It was only a few weeks since the funeral, when this house was filled with fellow Amish farmers, the ground between the house and barn filled with near-identical closed-top carriages, the barn filled with horses covered by handmade blankets. The pole, a good fifteen feet long crafted from the heartwood of a maple he and his father had taken down two years ago, was out of place. It was for pulling hay from the loft down to the horses and Benedict and his friends had needed it on visitation day so often that someone, probably Benedict himself, had merely propped it next to the door to the house. It was careless and lazy, undisciplined. Benedict knew his father would not have stood for such sloppiness in his only son, first-born, and now head of what remained of his family. He carried the pole back over to the barn.

Levi and Jacob, his father's closest friends since childhood, had visited today, along with Jacob's wife, Mary. The men had brought in the last of the corn and loaded it into the husker while Mary helped Felicity finish the day's housecleaning chores. The house at least was warmed by the wood stove while the barn was warmed only by the horses, his family's three bays along with the two that brought his friends for the day. They were gone now, the work done. Benedict walked to the rear of the building, past the stalls to the open area housing the moldboard and sulky plows and the seed drill and harrow. Across from those was the hay loft. He positioned the barrow beneath the opening in the slanted ceiling and reached up with the hook to pull hay down. It would be the final feed for his bays for the night, then he would pour fresh seed out for the chickens and pellets for the rabbits in their hutches. Then he could finish his day. He was dressed for fall weather but it was getting colder faster than he had expected today.

Not enough hay lay over the drop hole. He cursed for a few seconds, followed by the prayer for forgiveness. It had become more frequent, this momentary litany, since the accident that killed both his father and mother. The thought of it clouded his vision and made his eyes sting. It was not a good thing, he thought, this anger. A pair of young men, non-Amish, in that pickup truck at dusk, speeding heedlessly down the blacktop as his parents returned from their trip to the Perry's only a half-mile north to deliver sweet potatoes and pick up freshly harvested squash. A small obligation fulfilled at the cost of their lives. The carriage was mostly destroyed, with scars of yellow paint on the hub of the left rear axle that suggested the men may have dodged his parents at the last second and scraped the rear wheel, throwing the carriage off the road and into the ditch and windrow. That was their story. Benedict, when he saw the men at the police station, could see in their eyes that it was a lie, that they had done what drivers had done for decades: had wanted to scare his parents by passing them as closely as possible, even touching the axle. It was a game among the English of this part of the country. There was no doubt in his mind the men had recklessly killed his parents and that they would escape justice. It was always how these stories ended.

All horrifying, especially to his sister, barely able to care for herself, much less the household, before her parents' death. She had cried out for her mother without stopping for a day and a half when he took her in his arms and told her her parents were gone to heaven and would not come back. Since then, for weeks, she had been almost entirely silent, unwilling to speak of it and barely willing to eat or clean herself. Benedict was all she had, her good brother, at twenty four barely a year older than she, and he had to tear her from his embrace over and over since then, just to be able to go take care of things, to do the lonely work to provide for them both now. All joy had left their lives and every moment was painful in some way or another, even with help from their church and neighbors.

Benedict went back to the front of the barn and pulled the tall door closed. It was quite dark now and getting cold. Not cold enough to light the kerosene heater hanging from the center rafter, but it soon would be. He went into the alcove next to the doors and flipped two switches to the bank of batteries stacked against the wall. Small twelve-volt lights came on in sections of the barn, including two in the loft. He went out and climbed the wood ladder built into the wall next to the first stall, up to the loft. He carefully walked the double planking the length of the barn to the wall of hay stacked just inside the field door. He pulled down several bales and cut the strings with the small curved knife he kept on his belt. He shook the first bale loose and kicked it down the slope onto the drop hole. The rest he would have to do from below.

Just as he turned to go down the ladder at that end of the barn, he heard the squeal of the front door hinge. It could be his sister or the wind. When he descended to the dirt floor, he turned to look at the door. He froze at the silhouette of a man standing just inside the door. "Hello," he said. It wasn't quite a shout, but the barn was large and tall. "Who's there? Levi? Jacob? Did you forget something?"

MARTIN STOPPED when he heard the voice. He hadn't expected anyone to be in the barn. He turned around and stepped back through the door. He stood just behind it, waiting. Then he stepped back a couple of steps and to his right enough to see the man in the barn approaching him. No point in leaving, he told himself. He hadn't done anything. He just needed some gas.

The man was walking toward him faster now. "Hey!" the man said. "What do you want?"

Martin didn't speak for a moment. He was considering what to say. "Gas," he finally grunted. But the man hadn't heard him. As the man came up to the barn door and stepped out, Martin repeated, "Gas."

"Gas?" said the man now. He was slim, not much older than Martin, wearing clean overalls and a wool hat and good boots. There wasn't enough light to see much else.

"My truck," Martin said, pointing behind him with his stretched out arm. "Out of gas. You got some?"

The man stopped and watched Martin. "Not really. Chainsaw gas is all I have and it's got oil mixed in with it. Probably wouldn't be good for your motor."

"Okay," said Martin. "Better than nothing. I'm trying to get home."

"Where's home?" said the man.

"Wolf's Point."

"What's your name?"

"Martin. Conrad." Martin felt odd having given his name. Why would the man want to know that?

The man standing in the door of the barn said nothing. He seemed to be considering what to do. Finally he said, "Do you have a can you can put gas in? You can walk on down to Will Charon's farm, about a half mile on the left. He'll likely have gas for you. He uses a tractor and has a car."

Martin made a face. "Half a mile? You won't give me some gas? That's a long way and I'm getting real cold out here."

"Sir, I just don't have enough gas on hand, and like I told you, it's the wrong kind."

"Can you take me down to that other farm maybe? Bring me back to my truck?" "I'm sorry, I can't help you. That would mean harnessing my bay and pulling my small buggy out. I mean, I don't want to be uncharitable, but I have chores and my sister to take care of. I can't just leave her."

Martin felt his face flush and his pulse rise. He hadn't expected someone to refuse to help him. He glared for a moment without speaking. Then, "C'mon, just give me some of your gas. I don't want to hurt you but I will if I have to. I just want to get home and get warm."

The man in the door stiffened and stood up straighter. He put his hand on the handle of what might be a knife in a leather sheath on his belt. Martin took a step back, then stopped. His father hadn't taught him much, but he had told Martin to stand his ground if he felt he was in danger. It had seemed stupid advice to him at the time. He was shivering. It must be the cold, he thought. He couldn't walk away if there was any way he could find help.

The man in the barn took a step toward Martin. "Don't do that," Martin said, his voice low now, and gruff.

"Go on," said the man. "I told you I can't help you. Get out of here. Now."

Martin raised his hand, palm out. He looked hard at the man coming toward him and he felt a tightness starting in his groin and shooting up his spine. "Don't!"

Then something happened Martin hadn't expected. The man collapsed as if his legs had turned to rubber. He shook all over hard as Martin watched, not moving. As the man fell, it was as if he were an accordion that had lost its air. The top part of him, his chest and shoulders and arms and head, just drooped down onto his legs, which were folded oddly beneath him. Martin heard gurgling coming from the man's mouth and watched as the man vomited.

Martin looked at his hand, then looked down at the oddly shaped body. He hadn't made this happen, best he knew. He hadn't willed it, he was sure. The man just collapsed, nothing to do with him. But he had watched the man's face as he collapsed. He knew that no matter what, he would never get that image out of his mind. The man no longer looked human, but his eyes expressed fear, and confusion, and something far beyond both. Martin turned and walked away from the gurgling, shaking mass in front of the barn door, breathing hard. Then something Martin had no words for happened to him. It was as if he were two people in two places, one there on the ground, turning to get away, shaking with confusion himself, and another version of himself floating high above, looking down at the scene. Martin seemed to be inside this one, and he was calm. This one was trying to figure out what the one below should do now. But Martin could hardly think at all. He didn't know where to go. No point in going back to his dead truck. It was completely dark now. He was cold, so cold, almost shaking with it. He walked toward the house with its soft glowing light coming from the windows and door on this side. At least he could get warm there. Maybe he could call someone to pick him up. Maybe someone there would know what he needed to do. Maybe he would wake up from this nightmare. He didn't know anything. Maybe was all he had.

Beth Williams had just finished breakfast after feeding her son Jasper and her daughter Eli and packing them off to the school bus. She was dressing for her day at the hospital when she got the call from Matt Bettman, the Moniteau County sheriff. "We need you this morning up on 87. It's an Amish farmhouse, I'll send you the address when I have it. Drive on up, you'll see the lights."

"Okay. Got to call the hospital, tell them where I'm going. See you in a few minutes." About two miles north of Prairie Home she saw flashing lights. When she pulled into the long gravel drive of the Petersheim home, she found the sheriff's black F-150 with it's narrow strip of lights on the roof, along with two Moniteau County squad cars and a state police muscle car. They had left room for Beth in her SUV loaded with coroner's gear. She walked over to four men in uniforms standing in a circle near the barn.

Matt offered her a cup of coffee from his thermos.

"You know you men are tramping on my evidence, right?" she said, accepting the cup with a grimace. "What do we have?"

"We're hoping you'll be able to tell us," said Matt, the tallest and stockiest of the lot. He was in his fifties, hair cropped close to the sides of his head and turning gray from the bottom up. Former Marine style. "One fatality, male, mid-twenties we think. You remember the Amish man and wife killed when they were run off the road about a month ago? Their son. Now he's dead, in a heap over there just this side of the barn door. I'm pretty sure no one's touched him and we didn't move anything. We got the call from a cell phone. Two young men, they say they're the victim's friends, they found him when they came over this morning to work with him. Farming jobs, they say, but I haven't finished interviewing them." He paused, grimaced, sipped his coffee. "Beth, none of us seen anything like this before. Not even in Afghanistan. We can't figure out what happened to this guy. Maybe you can."

Beth didn't say anything. She walked to the collapsed body – she couldn't come up with any better word for what she was looking at. She didn't see any blood, though she'd have to lift the body to be sure. He lay on a clay-gravel mix, so it could have soaked up anything coming from the body. But the position of the body – Matt was right. She'd never seen anything like this either.

Back to her SUV, she opened the back and pulled out a drawer from one of the several racks of equipment. She unfolded a white body suit, mask and booties to go over her shoes. Then she opened the metal case containing her camera and batteries and memory cards. She stopped by Matt on her way back to the body. "Go ahead and call an ambulance, will you? I'll need to take the body back to my lab before I can give you anything useful."

MATT KNEW BETH would take her time, start with photos taken from all angles. Then she'd examine the body and ground as thoroughly as possible and have the EMTs load the body. There was nothing he could do now but get in the way. He went over to the house where his newest deputy, Marilyn, 20, just out of training, sat with two Amish men and the vic's sister. Each time Matt was around Marilyn, he couldn't help thinking she seemed too good looking to be a good policeman. On the other hand, maybe that just meant he was getting to old to be a good policeman.

He tried to recall the victim's sister's name. He pulled out the little note pad in his outside left jacket pocket and flipped pages until he found today's notes: Felicity.

She and Marilyn sat across from each other at the kitchen table. They were pretty close to the same age, Matt thought, and similar in other ways: both fair haired and thin. Marilyn was wiry at least, and strong. She had had no trouble finishing the physical part of her training, which had surprised Matt a little. He didn't want to be sexist, but he had initially doubted the girl could keep up in a demanding situation. He hadn't really tested her yet, but he really didn't want to have to. At his age, even though he wasn't fat and still had good legs, he knew the girl could probably outrun him like a gazelle. Fast reflexes too, enough to stay ahead of most bad guys she might run into. She was fairly cute too, more than most women academy grads from the county. But that wasn't why he had hired her.

Felicity, though. She was not just thin. She was gaunt. Matt had seen young Afghan women like her, bone and skin, with blank looks and fingers like claws. Starved, mostly. Looking around the kitchen, that wasn't likely the case for the daughter of this family, even though her parents had died. There was plenty of food. She just didn't look like she was eating much of it.

And now this. He sat down between his deputy and Felicity. "Miss," he began, looking at her. She didn't look back. She stared at her hands. "Miss?"

Still no response. "Felicity?" he said, a little louder. She turned her head toward him, but with a vague look to her, as if she were looking for the source of the sound.

"Felicity, I'm Sheriff Bettman. I need to ask you some questions. Are you up for that? That okay right now?"

He waited, thinking he was going to have to take her in, get a social worker in the room, or maybe her minister.

"Do you have any other family around here?"

After a beat, as if it took a while for his words to reach her brain and even longer for her brain to process what he had said, she finally looked up at him and shook her head. No family.

"You're Amish, right? Yes? Can you give me the name of your minister?"

Marilyn cleared her throat and handed Matt a card. "This was taped to their refrigerator. Deacon Milliner. There's no phone number but there's an address."

"Okay. Thanks. Miss? Do you want me to get hold of this deacon of yours? Maybe he can be of some comfort." To his surprise, Felicity spoke.

"He came in here. Said he wanted to use a telephone. We don't have a telephone. He was mad. Real mad, and shaking. Then he came at me. Said he wanted to hold me. I said go away, get away! He pushed me, hard." She was in tears. Her voice soft, she said, "Then he told me to take off my dress. I screamed for Benedict but the man said he wouldn't be able to help me. He was horrible, saying to take off my clothes. I ran into my bedroom and locked the door. He didn't get in. He didn't try. Then I didn't hear him anymore. I yelled some more for my brother, but he never came home. I didn't come out until this girl knocked on my door this morning and said she was the police."

"So you saw this man? Felicity, this is important. What did he look like? Would you recognize him if you saw him again?"

She was in tears now, her head on the table in her hands. "Go away. Please. I need to lay down now."

Marilyn rose and took Felicity's shoulders and guided her to her room. She glanced back at her boss. She mouthed, "Later, okay?" Matt nodded. It had been a stupid question anyway. Of course she would recognize her attacker. The killer. But he needed a description.

BACK OUTSIDE, MATT NOTICED a second state trooper vehicle in the lot. The trooper stood chatting with the small knot of officers. One of them pointed to him and the guy walked over to him. "Sheriff Bettman? I'm officer Charles. Raymond Charles. People always think my last name is my first ... anyway, I thought you'd want to know we found a pickup truck, an older model Ford, about half a mile north on the highway. We don't know if it's connected to what happened here or not. It might just be that a farmer left it there. It's got an old field tag, so we might be able to identify the owner. But I doubt it. Vehicles like this trade hands informally all the time. But I thought you might want to know about it." Matt pulled out a pack of Marlboro's and offered the officer one. "No sir, I don't smoke," he said. He pulled a face like who the hell smokes anymore, are you trying to kill yourself? Everyone Matt knew did that to him. He lit up anyway.

"Thanks Charles. Ray. Like the singer? You must get a lot of that. Good to know. We'll check it out anyway. We have a real mysterious death here so we'll be checking everything." The officer nodded and returned to his vehicle and, and after a brief word to his colleague, pulled out. Farm truck, Matt thought. If it's out of gas, maybe someone walked down here from it, looking for gas. He turned to his deputy. "Hey Jerry. Go see if there are any gas cans out. I'm wondering if someone tried to get some here."

"He's Amish, Matt. They don't use gas for their machinery."

"Go look anyway."

MATT FOLLOWED BETH WILLIAMS' SUV down to the hospital in the county seat. He knew he would be a nuisance, that Beth wouldn't be able to tell him much, but he wasn't ready to go back to his office just yet. He didn't have much to work with. The body was his best clue – maybe his only clue. There was Felicity though. He had called the highway patrol main office in Jefferson City, the state capital, to send a sketch artist up to her. She had seen the assailant, and maybe when she was calmer, she would be able to tell him more. But he doubted it. She struck him as completely unable to care for herself. Maybe even be mentally incapacitated. At least she had escaped her brother's fate.

He parked in back of the hospital and went down the ramp to the basement door. The ambulance was pulling out, having already wheeled the body to Beth's lab. "I won't stay long," he said, when she came out of her office in scrubs. She busied herself positioning the overhead cameras. Matt noticed she was careful not to look at the twisted lump that covered half of her autopsy table.

"That's good because I won't have much for you for a while. It'll probably be tonight sometime before I can send you the slideshow."

"Yeah. Still. Just some general observations? I need something to work with when I get back to my desk."

She stepped over to the left side of the body and lifted the arm. "All right. No rigor mortis." She lifted the eyelids of the misshapen head. "I'd guess death was more than sixteen hours ago." Her foot tapped a button on the floor to start recording. She walked around the body, lifting and observing. "From the shape and position of the body, it looks like every bone in it was broken. In fact, ..." she stopped, looking at the shoulders and then the hips, "Matt, this is way beyond odd. Look at this." She lifted the body more or less to its side and stroked the area of at the top of the buttocks. "The shape of his pelvis, it's just wrong. Even with his clothes on, see how flat this is? The ilium, this part of the hip, it should stick out. We should be able to feel it clearly here." She reached down and tapped the top of her hip on the side. "This bone is shaped more or less like a bowl. But his .... it's flat. Like it's been bent. Or not bent – flattened somehow.

"Matt, that's just not possible."

The sheriff stared at the place where he knew the bone should protrude. The flesh was rounded, sunk in. For a moment it was hard to think of the mass he was looking at as human, it was so unnatural.

"Why impossible?"

"It's a large bone, especially dense there. And brittle. Enough force on it would break it, oh, down here somewhere," Beth drew an imaginary line across the middle of her hip with a finger. "It would snap if you put enough pressure on it. But it would take a lot more than any one person could apply. And if it were hit with a blunt object with enough mass, it would shatter that bone. This one, best I can tell, is ..., it's just ...." She probed the area of the corpse with three fingers. "Jesus, Matt. It's there, I can feel bone, it's just flat and it feels ... pebbly. Rough. Not at all natural. I've got to get this body X-rayed before I do much else. Why don't you go on. I'll send you the images as soon as I get them, okay?" She looked up at the sheriff. Matt could tell she wanted him to leave. This was going to be a hard one. She needed room breathe, time to think. They both did.

"Thanks Beth. Call me if you need anything." He didn't know what else to say, so he turned to the door and left her to her job.

MATT DECIDED TO GO BACK to the crime scene. He drove the twenty-five miles up route 87 slowly. He needed time to think, to let this whole thing sink in. Ever since he came to Moniteau County over thirty years ago and hired on as a deputy, right out of college and the police academy, he'd never seen a case as strange as this one. Murders, sure, but they had all been similar in one way or another. Often the result of a domestic dispute, or alcoholic stupidity, or just plain clumsiness. It was part of rural life that people got jacked on drugs or booze and went at each other for one damned reason or another. City life, too, he supposed, though his whole career had been in the county. Country life suited him. The quiet, the vistas and trees, though in this part of the state it was more rolling hills and tree lines bordering creeks and corn fields. Still, it settled his nerves to look across those fields at occasional houses and barns and implements. It was why he spent a lot of his time in his truck, crackling police radio the background music to his job, driving endless blacktops between small towns. Cruising the gravel side roads too, enjoying the crunching of gravel under his Michelins, scanning everything, trying to notice what had changed, who was who, in what, after all this time, he felt was his territory. County sheriff. Running mostly unopposed every few years. He never even thought about moving up, moving out. He had the experience, and due to constant reading and training, could have had a gold star by now in one of the city departments up north.

He drove past the Petersheim mailbox, looking for that old pickup the trooper had mentioned. He found it about a half mile on up, on the left side. It was headed south and parked half on the gravel shoulder and half on the grass next to the ditch. He pulled a U-turn and pulled in behind it.

It had been another half-mile or so north of this that Benedict and Felicity's parents were killed by those two Booneville boys, driving reckless down this highway, not paying attention, high on weed and meth. They were out on bail now, which just felt wrong to Matthew, but there was nothing he could do but see them in court when their case came up in a few months. They said they tried get around the Petersheim's horse and buggy and claimed the carriage was across the line and they didn't have enough room to miss them. But lack of skid marks and damage to the right side of their car told another story. He'd seen it before in this part of the county. Kids trying to see how close they could get to the buggy wheel to scare the Amish couple and their horse. Well, they'd done that all right. Scared them right off the road and into the stumps of ash trees that made up the fence on the west side. The carriage had shattered, along with the horse and old man and his wife.

Matt got out and walked up to the truck. There were no keys, but the door was unlocked. No way to start it and check the gas gauge. Still, the perp might have run out here and walked down to the Petersheim's. Their drive was the closest to the truck. His deputy, Jerry, had reported there were two small cans of gasoline in a room in the barn next to a chainsaw. Both full. So if the perp had shown up looking for gas for this truck, he must have left without finding it, or decided not to go back to the truck.

But he didn't just run. He went in the house and scared the dickens out of Felicity. After that he must have walked off. Or maybe caught a ride with someone. He examined the truck bed: empty beer cans, quite old. No sign of any new ones there or in the cab. Nothing else suggesting the guy was on something. If he had been high on weed, there likely would have been seeds or leaf particles on the floor or in the crack of the seat. Matt found that often enough when he stopped people. Though weed was hardly evidence that the guy was high enough to be a danger to himself or anyone else. Dirt though, plenty of that all over. Cakes of mud. That too was common enough to ignore. After all, the truck didn't have any plates. From the looks of it, old, mostly worn out, with grass and mud in the bed and on floor of the cab, it must be what folks around the county called a 'farm truck', meaning it wasn't registered at all, or hadn't been for a long time. Often used to haul people and gear to the fields and back. Strictly speaking, these were supposed to be registered with the state and carry a special license plate, but farmers only really did that for certain large trucks meant to pull field implements and rolls of hay on the highway.

Matt collected the VIN of the truck, shut the door, and returned to his truck. That patrolman, what was his name? Like the musician. Ray Charles ... he likely had done a search on the VIN to see who last registered it. He'd have to give the Highway Patrol center a call.

On his way back down the highway to the Petersheim place, his phone rang. It was Beth.

"Hi Matt. I sent the x-ray images and photos of the body over to your office e-mail. But I wanted to tell you something I found. You're not driving, are you? Got a minute?"

He pulled into the Petersheim's drive and stopped. "Yeah, go ahead. I'm parked. What you got?"

"Well, it's hard to explain. Matt, this is weirder than I thought. A whole different kind of weird. You ready for this?"

"Just tell me."

"When I opened him up, everything was normal and I didn't find any trauma. Except his bones. You know I told you his pelvis was flattened? Turns out all of his bones were wrong. Shaped wrong. A lot of them broken. Maybe that's not the right word. More like they had dissolved and then refused. But refused in the wrong shape."

"Refused? What does that mean?"

"You know when you break a bone, and you get it set and it heals? Well, the parts that were broken grow back together. That refusing. It always produces extra calcium around the break, at least some. Now imagine you somehow crushed a bone, I mean completely crushed it so it was in thousands of very small pieces. Now imagine that bone was never set, never positioned so it would grow back into its original shape, but it refused itself anyway.

"Matt, best I can tell in a partial autopsy, that's what every bone in this man's body did. Crushed into tiny pieces, then rejoined, but so fast there's no evidence of extra calcium. It's like all his bones fell apart and then became solid again, at least most of it. Best I've been able to tell, that's what killed him. His organs couldn't take the strain of being in the wrong positions in his body, because his skeleton no longer held them in correctly. The pressure on his heart alone would have killed him in less than a minute."

Matt held the phone to his ear, trying to imagine what Beth had described.

"Beth, I ..." he began. But he didn't know what to tell her. "So ... you've never seen anything like this, right? Has anyone? Have you scanned the literature? The Internet?"

"Yes, Matt, I have." Impatience in her voice. She was a professional, despite her youth. "There are no mentions of anything like this. I even put a call into an acquaintance at John Hopkins in Baltimore to call me so I can ask him if he has any idea what this is."

"Jeeze, Beth. Okay. Good work." Then he had a sudden thought. "Do you think there's any chance this could be caused by some kind of, I don't know, virus or something? Something biological?"

"I don't know, Matt. But I'm going to quarantine this body until I know more." There was silence on the line. Matt could hear Beth breathing hard.

"Take it easy there, okay sweetheart? I'll be back pretty soon. We can talk over next steps then." Matt clicked the OFF button. He had meant to check on Felicity. He hoped someone, her minister likely, had taken charge of her. He would check on her later. Instead, he pulled his truck around in the yard in front of the barn and headed south on the highway.

The moment Beth heard the line go dead after updating Matt, she had two immediate thoughts. One, she would have to talk to Matt about his language. She knew he meant nothing by it, but still. It's not right to call a colleague "sweetheart," not these days. It would embarrass them both for her to bring it up, but she liked Matt. He was one of the good ones, didn't have a bad bone in his body, and it might help him, maybe even save his career, if he knew how dangerous it was to assume things about women.

Second, it occurred to her she knew someone closer she could call who might be able to help her with this corpse problem. She had taken a course in forensics from Eve Sheffield at the University of Missouri in Columbia last year. Eve had become her friend and had even helped her secure her job with Moniteau County as medical examiner, even though the county commissioners considered her young and inexperienced and a woman. She could call Eve. If anyone in the area could help her explain what had happened to this man, Eve would be able to, and she was quite sure Eve would be interested. Interested! Unless she was badly mistaken, this case was one for the books.

Beth glanced down at the handy foot-switches to the side of her table. She tapped the one for making phone calls and spoke to the microphone hanging over the table. "Call Eve Sheffield," she said. She knew the AI in her system would know how to handle the request. "Calling Eve Sheffield," she heard the soft female voice respond, followed by the dial tone and ten musical notes. After a few seconds, she heard, "You've reached the office of Eve Sheffield. I can't come to the phone right now. Please leave me a message."

After the beep, Beth said, "Eve! This is Beth Williams over in Moniteau County. I have a pretty strange case here that I'm sure you'll want to see." Then her cell number and another tap on the foot-switch to hang up the call, and Beth stepped back to the corpse to continue her inspection.

SHERIFF BETTMAN checked into his office after leaving Beth at the morgue. There were no messages. He thought he should research this odd killing up on 87, but when he sat down and opened his browser, he couldn't think what search terms to put in. He stared at the screen, then down at his desktop: there were no other current cases, a good thing. The work was getting done. But this case — a whopper. He knew he'd have to get a better interview with the Petersheim girl, if possible. He stepped out into the main room looking for Marilyn. She was by her desk, putting lotion on her hands. Takes care of herself, that woman does, he thought. Someone's going to snatch her up pretty fast, make her a housewife maybe. Then I'll have to hunt up another recruit. Or maybe she won't do that — maybe she'll turn out to be dedicated. Then she might ripen into a real policewoman. Matt could only hope.

He walked up to her. "What's the story with the Amish girl? Did her deacon ever show up? Is she still at her home? I asked the state police in Jeff to send me a sketch artist. We need to get a description."

"I called him, yes. A Deacon Oran Milliner," she said, checking her notebook. "It turns out she does have family in Clark, an uncle. Milliner said he would take her up there to stay with his family. He's supposed to call me with an address."

"That's better than leaving her by herself in that house, surrounded by ghosts. But we need to know where she is and we need to get that artist to her. If you don't get an address today, I want you to drive up to Clark tomorrow morning and ask around until you find her, and bring her down here."

Marilyn didn't look happy, but she nodded. "If we bring her in, we'll need to contact state social services to send someone to be with her here."

"Whatever. That'll cost us, but we have to have a description. Thanks Marilyn."

Matt headed toward the front door. He nodded to his dispatcher, Karen. "Going to lunch," he said.

 the Nick-Nak, Matt found a table and ordered breaded pork steak, hash browns and coffee. It was the kind of meal his ex-wife had always refused to make for him. You're already overweight, she said whenever he ordered fried potatoes when eating out. You want to kill yourself with a heart attack? Dammit. She had left him, but that voice in his head wouldn't go away. But it was his comfort food. And today, with a case like this one, he wasn't going to order a damn salad for lunch.

He heard a ding and felt a vibration at his waist. He wasn't used to his new cell phone but it came with the job. At least he didn't have to pay for it, or the service. He lifted it from the holster it was in and looked at it. It was an LG something, the phone, with a large black screen surrounded by a tough plastic case, red and black with ribbing to protect it if dropped.

He tapped the face of it twice with his finger. A white strip in the middle indicated he had an email. The subject line said "Report on Truck". Matt swiped up and connected four of the white dots that appeared with the security pattern he had created when he got the phone. From the home page, he touched the white icon with the large "M" in it to open Gmail.

It was from the state trooper who had spotted the old truck north of the Petersheim's. "No record of inspection or re-registration of that truck in over 15 years," the message read. "But a fellow trooper tells me it looks like one he used to see pretty often on 87 between 179 and Jamestown. He's not sure, but the driver could be a construction worker who has an old bulldozer he stores in a lot in Jamestown. Sorry, that's best I can do." It was signed "Officer Ray Charles, Missouri State Highway Patrol."

Not much, Matt thought to himself, but better than nothing. He took his time with lunch, savoring the crunch and flavor of potatoes fried in hot oil. When finished, he went out to his truck and pulled out the handset and clicked it to contact his dispatcher. "Karen, I'm going up to Jamestown to check out a lead," he said.

He'd have to thank Ray Charles, he told himself. Especially if his information leads to anything useful. He started up his F-150 and headed north.

CHAPTER TWO

Miraculous Mother

ANNA MARIE HOPE, like most girls her age, was no stranger to confusion and disorientation. But returning to her room at Sarah Lawrence College from the student health center, she found she had to work harder than usual to hold her focus and not fall as she walked. She had gone because of unexpected nausea each morning this week. Pregnant! It didn't seem possible. She didn't remember having sex with anyone in the last few months. She was surprised and annoyed with herself to say the least. She was current with her birth control pills, she was pretty sure. And it wasn't like she was sexually active. The last time – the only time really that this could have happened – was the night she had gone with Zoe to a Dave Matthews concert and after, they went to their favorite bar and there he was, this guy, a student in one of her classes. They had had about two shots too many and she might have gone with him to his apartment. When she woke the next morning, groggy and disoriented, she still had her panties and bra on. He was gone. She dressed and went back to her place. She didn't remember anything happening. She assumed they'd had sex.

The concert had been at the end of the first semester of Anna's final year. An early celebration of the successful conclusion of her college career. The graduation ceremony at the end of May was coming all too soon. She had to decide: keep this baby or not?

The not-option was easy enough. The girls here talked about it all the time. It seemed like every other week the whisper was about one of them "going down to Brooklyn". But the only thing Anna knew for sure was that she was determined not to be like all the other princesses here, not to go from Sarah Lawrence to cocktail parties in the city to meet wealthy traders, hook up, have huge weddings, kids, homes in the Hamptons and Florida and maybe Italy, and age gracefully playing bridge with her former classmates on Thursday nights.

She didn't want to decide, actually. She didn't tell anyone about the growing life in her belly, especially her parents. She knew her mother would want her to get rid of it. It would become the only thing she talked about. Worse, her mother would likely come to New York and arrange the whole thing, take the decision out of Anna's hands – or her uterus – completely. Anna couldn't allow that, that much she knew. Concentrating on getting herself to classes daily, studying and writing intensively – she wouldn't let this defeat her determination to succeed at her studies (that was her dad's side of her, it occurred to her), she looked up one morning and realized her decision was made: she was past the legal period for an abortion in New York. She toughed it out through the semester. When the only thing left was to prepare for the perp-walk across the stage to shake hands with the president and collect that damn diploma, she realized she would be six months along, her usual slim, fit self bulging in the middle, showing, and her parents would be out there, watching. It might not be obvious under her graduation robe, but they would arrive and give her hugs and then her pregnancy would no longer be secret. She would have to face the music.

The decision to skip graduation was easier than she expected. It was as if she knew all along what she was going to do. Like there had been whisperings in her head telling her to call her parents and let them know not to fly to New York, that she was going to drive back before the ceremony.

When classes were over she packed all her belongings into her Range Rover and drove west, toward the land of her birth, a tall coffee in its holder, and with a mixtape blasting from her Smart Radio. She hadn't bothered to let her parents know she was on the road.

When she reached Indiana, she began to wonder what she was doing. Was she really going to go back to her life in Lake Forest, have this baby, turn her life back over to her mother who would hire a nanny while Anna lounged with her friends around the pool, went for outings on her dad's sailboat, having nothing else to do but chatter with mindless friends about fashion and who was this week's scandal in their tight little village?

When she reached Indianapolis, she pulled over at the intersection of 70 and 65. She calmed her breathing and after a toilet break, she considered her options. As had been happening since the beginning of her pregnancy, she heard whispers in her head: keep going west, it said. It felt different to Anna, not really like her own thoughts. But whatever it was, she listened and agreed. Back in her SUV, she continued west on I-70. If she were going to go home, she would have an opportunity again in Illinois, at highway 57.

When she reached Effingham, faced with the decision

again, the whispered voice felt even more urgent. It would be a failure to go north, it said to her, back to her mother's smothering nest, back to the fluff of her privileged life. She listened. She agreed. She continued west.

It was like a stone had lifted from her chest when she reached St. Louis. On west then, the voice said. She had no idea where she might end up, but it wouldn't be the gated community north of Chicago. Maybe Colorado? Or California? She sighed at the prospect. She had already been driving for almost twenty hours. What would it take to get to San Francisco? Three more days? The voice returned. Not there, it seemed to say. Somewhere much closer.

She kept going, listening to the voice in her mind, feeling her way, trusting her instincts.

Halfway across the state of Missouri she reached Columbia. Ravenous after the long drive, she went down to the center of the university town. It had, to her eyes, a tiny downtown, but it seemed to sparkle with the energy of the students walking about and lounging on the sidewalks in front of colorful boutique shops. She pulled her Range Rover into a slanted parking spot on Broadway near a guitar player sitting on a planter filled with bougainvilleas, his instrument case open at his feet with a few one dollar bills in it. She got out and brushed her hair.

"Hi. I'm looking for a good place to eat. Any suggestions?"

"Vegetarian or meat?" he replied. Anna thought about it for a moment. She wasn't vegetarian, strictly speaking, but after too many hours of driving, too much loud music, too much coffee, her stomach seemed to say 'take it easy on me please'.

"Vegetarian, I think."

The musician pointed down the cross street where he was located. Ninth street. "About a block down on your left. Called Main Squeeze. Can't miss it."

She smiled, said thanks and dropped a fiver in his guitar case. Then she walked down to her lunch, one of the best she had ever had, as it turned out.

Later, after exploring several charming shops on Ninth for a while, she returned to her car. She considered whether this town might be her destination. It was a comfortable, charming place. So much smaller than what she was used to either in Illinois or in New York, but so much more personable. A sweet mix of culture and intelligent company and accessibility. Anna sat in her car and quieted her breathing. Listen, she told herself. Listen to the voice. You'll know what to do next.

She found her way back out to interstate 70 and continued her oddessy west. After what seemed only a few minutes, she found herself crossing a bridge over a wide river: the Missouri. What a sight! The biggest river she had ever seen. Wide and brown, hugging its shore on both sides, with tall limestone cliffs on the east and wide fields on the west. She was surprised that, despite its size, she could glimpse water moving with a force far beyond anything she had seen before. So much power! Anna slowed as much as she could safely and decided she wanted to see more of this river.

Where though?

About a mile up the road, the first exit offered her an opportunity. Stopping at the top of the exit ramp, she checked her Google map. Driving south should take her near the river. The first town, Wooldridge, appeared to be right next to it.

It was, but reaching the river turned out to be a problem. It was on the other side of a wide field of corn, with barely a dirt road crossing it, hidden behind a row of trees.

Another look at Google Map showed another, possibly better, access point to the river on down the road. After a half hour, she was able to see the river in the distance, behind more trees, mist giving it a mysterious, looming presence. She dropped down a long hill like a roller coaster into a tiny town called Wolf's Point. It was a village, population 29, so said a sign at the bottom of the hill, with perhaps a couple dozen modest houses and a church. She drove onto blacktop and gravel streets past what looked like a general store and the ruins of an old bank leading to the river. She stopped twenty feet past some railroad tracks, got out, and was amazed at the sight of the river, not ten feet below where she stood.

She couldn't estimate its width, she discovered. Partly because of the mist hanging over it, partly because looking across it, it seemed endless. She could see a vague line of light green trees and bushes on the opposite shoreline but to her right and left, the river and the skyline merged seamlessly. Though it seemed to flow fairly slowly, she guessed that too was an illusion. This much water, moving at any speed, was immeasurable, relentless, an unstoppable force.

She frowned as it occurred to her that her years of classes in literature and her efforts as a creative writer meant her ability to see the river as it actually was must be hampered by her habits of abstracting things. In one sense, the river wasn't a river: it was a metaphor. A moving mass, unstoppable under any circumstances. Like life, it was unknowable, unpredictable, and magnificent.

I think too much, she said to herself. But it was her way. All her life Anna had longed to express – something. The story of her life, or of a life, in such a way that no one could miss the universal connections to their own story. This river is the connection, she felt, the story of all of us, of life itself. In addition to motherhood, this was an inspiration and opportunity to try tell such a story.

As she stood looking at the river, she felt the voice in her head again. Yes, it seemed to say, this is the place. She was sure now that this tiny town, this village, was where she would take a stand, to find herself, as her grandmother used to say to her when she was a girl. Now she need to find a way to stay here.

She started looking. It took only moment to find a house, empty and abandoned, not much more than a shell of a place, partially built and then abandoned. She could set up camp, cozy down and shelter herself and her child to come while she waited for a better home to appear. When she found it, she knew her father would understand and help her if she needed it.

Meanwhile, this would serve as base camp for her next adventure: the exploration and discovery of what it means to be Anna Marie Hope.

IT WAS AUGUST, the hottest, sweatiest time here in the middle of the United States. And the middle of the night too. Again as so many times these last three months, Anna opened the sagging screen door of this ragged unfinished house and ran through the too-high grass and weeds to the outhouse door. Where am I? Who am I now? Her thoughts flew fast and in all directions these days. Wealthy parents, top student at Sarah Lawrence College, she was used to guiding her galloping thoughts the way she used to ride her favorite gelding, controlling and directing it despite its bursting, youthful energy. But now, late summer, hot and alone in this verdant wilderness by this massive river, who was she? Even now in the dark, squatting over this wooden hole, she could hear it behind her, feel its force like a current running through her mind. She could feel it pushing on her too, in the form of this swollen belly, this new child so near to its birth, restless and rippling beneath her flesh like the surface of that river, determined to flow forth from her. All of this amplified by the overpowering odor of old and new shit and piss and crumbling wood and rotting vegetation.

Raised a precious princess, sheltered in the blue light of Lake Forest society, summers on Lake Michigan yachts, bright (like her father), beautiful, as her mother must once have been. "Now look at me," she whispered, sitting in the cool of this dark box, peeing to relieve, just a little, the unending pressure of this child, alone in this odd place. Next to the old house she had found and moved into without asking. An empty, abandoned thing at one end of a tiny hamlet, doing a slow collapse into dust and splinters. Despite who she had been before this pregnancy and this flight to ... what? Despite no longer quite knowing herself, she somehow treasured this new life, this place, as well as this new little person growing within.

The moment she coasted down that long final hill to Wolf's Point and drove over the railroad tracks to the bank and looked out, she could feel it pulling on her. She may not have known where she was going, what to do with her life, but this river knew. There could be no questions regarding its direction and its force and authority. The moment she laid eyes on it, her breathing calmed in a way she had never known before.

Now, three months after Wolf's Point and the river grabbed her imagination, her life seemed a string of ragged moments defined by necessity: drive up to town, eat, come back, sleep a little, huddle under her grandmother's quilts, jump up and make her way to the outhouse in her dark flannel nightgown, ankles rubbed raw from running sockless in her boots, day and night running to that wooden slab door that opened to reveal the spoils of organic depredations, the harrowing black maw set among the ghostly dark within, assaulting her with a not entirely unpleasant draft of night soil, an odor that made her think of what it must smell like to be born or perhaps to die, especially on these early mornings, dawn only a dream or a hint, not yet even the sound of mourning doves waking the day.

It woke her though, these morning runs through tangled vegetation, wet with dew, and part of her welcomed that, the movements of her body, the chill of early morning air, coolness on her feet and ankles, warm breezes on her cheeks, the outdoors, though she wanted most of all to sleep more, if only such a thing could be possible. After lying awake all through the night, or nearly, the pressure pushed her up and out of her too-soft straw and cotton-wicked bed, a bit of a struggle to sit, while it was still dark.

She no longer tried to remember who she had been or even who this place might be making her into, or the time or place of what was to come, now, after these months of settling into a kind of day-time somnolence as she stirred porridge for breakfast, and made tea from the last of the chamomile and spearmint and lemon grass, stored in an old candy tin with rusted edges which she sometimes couldn't open without fishing out the screwdriver, itself rusted with a chewed-up handle that she had found in the far left kitchen drawer. Eyes closed, she slumped against the counter on an old stool covered with frayed gingham. Her kettle on her tiny propane stove whistled and she stirred herself.

Her cup of tea in hand, she pushed open the back door and picked up the shovel.

Did others remember her? Of course they must but she mostly didn't care, and cared even less in these moments about her neighbors living in the small houses on either side, or across the gravel road on the river side. Even the woman, so much heavier than she was and so much shorter too looking for all the world like a character in a Shakespearean play when she knocked twice and came in without waiting for a response, which was perhaps a neighbor woman's duty when visiting a young woman nine months pregnant and living alone. Adele, her name.

Would she ever really remember things again? Living alone, she said it again to herself, in these wilds, near abandoned farms and homesteads in the bottoms surrounded by swamps and creeks and trees that swayed like angry ghosts in the night, and the howling of coyote pups not a hundred feet away. So far from what she had known and had thought must be the world: the ease and comfort of her parents' home in Lake Forest, from the artificial luxurious pretense of poverty of Sarah Lawrence, her whole world for four years. Luxury so taken for granted that she had been barely aware of it. And now this. Still a kid, her mother would say, just out of school, but she didn't feel so young anymore. She felt a large, creaking, straining thing, nauseous much of the time, reviling and rejoicing in her own juices, with a head that would not stop whirling, swamped with thoughts and feelings. And a voice, urging her to continue. And this vagueness. This exhaustion.

ADELE WAS A CURIOUS WOMAN, maybe fifty, pudgy faced, a widow, fifth generation of her family she said (the only thing they had in common? Anna remembered her grandmother's stories about the exodus from the high plains of Russia) who had inherited her house with the worn wooden shutters and sagging porch across from Anna, and who, despite having been married for many years, despite her peasant girth and swarthy round cheeks and belly, had never borne a child.

Still, Anna felt somehow safer when Adele came, though she liked living alone, had wanted to live alone, had dreamed of it even before becoming pregnant and now that she was, was even more determined to see this through, just her and her child. It was the wildness she craved, she told herself, the rough space and even the heedlessness, even the splinters of the wood framing of her doors and windows, the dust and holes in the ancient cheap carpet. They fit her mind, her sense of her unfinished, retrograde self. Since she had arrived in this place she had been filled with a conviction that she was where she needed to be, a place so unlike where she came from that she could see her origins in a wholly new way, where she was destined to have new, and new kinds, of experiences she could tell her grandchildren about, as her grandmother had once hinted to her about the year she traveled the Klondike with her husband in endless snow and pain and effort and even the death of a friend of theirs, a man they had lived and traveled with. A story her grandmother laughed at each time she told it. Anna remembered looking into her grandmother's eyes then and seeing them coal black, though she knew they couldn't be, and the fierce joy her grandmother took in her memories, and the haunted look after, as she returned to her bitter reality, fingers twisting madly as she married needle to thread, quilting her refuge, married to a former miner and wildcatter who did little now, who rarely moved at all and almost never spoke. "Find yourself girl!" she had whispered to Anna. "Don't settle down too quickly!" Which Anna remembered as she grew and went to the expensive east coast school her mother insisted upon and her father seemed happy to pay for, remembering her grandmother and her fierce sadness and how a life can come to its close with nothing more than faint memories and a sense of self that's turned to smoke over time. She swore she would not have such a fate, that her fate would be what she made it, and it must not be made idly or easily or quickly. And so she worked hard and wrote furiously and poured her anger and fears and hopes into poetry and fiction and was accepted into that impossible school. That effort had done much to shape who she was now, made her think always about who she wanted to become, that memory of her grandmother. She had loved that unknowable hard edged woman with dark eyes, and feared her a little too.

Now, Anna felt gripped and annoyed by too much civilization each time she encountered it, even in the small towns near Wolf's Point when she went shopping. Her father had given her a bottomless credit card, but still she found herself puzzled and infuriated by the kind of people who preferred a passive, civilized life, who seemed to need it, who insisted on it and who seemed destined to be its victims. It all left her with a conviction of wrongness and of better ways, though despite the intelligence that had surrounded her for the last four years she could not visualize it. While at school, she had read all she could to try to discover what true living must be, what community could be if only people would choose to live it. Thoreau and Emerson and the Shakers and a particular favorite of her one of her teachers, the Chautauquas of the late 19th century, which she had studied and which had informed her graduation thesis. But nothing seemed to hold. There were always flaws, human failings and misunderstandings and worse, and until she found such people, a true community of peaceful and intelligent people who had somehow gotten past confusions and personal striving (and she secretly thought she might never find them), she would live alone. Self reliant, if not self sufficient.

IT WAS MID-AFTERNOON, the hottest part of this summer day, and Anna was sweating. She might as well be living in Hawaii, like her sister. She thought she must melt, there could be no relief for these moments but night, which, though she wished for it, came too soon because it was dusk before she felt wake enough and well enough to step outside and work on her projects, and then it went dark, rather quickly here because they were in a deep valley, and cooling breezes swept down the hills behind her and that was a relief and she worked on into the dark until she couldn't see. It was only a garden, a small one, and she only needed to turn some soil, cut it with the edge of her spade, step on it with one foot and push and sometimes it sank in cleanly and she was able to pull and push until the clod broke loose and she reached down to the base of the spade handle and lifted, grunting and still sweating and feeling the strain in her belly but also the breeze and lifting the dirt to the small pile next to her. Sometimes the spade would not cut through, it would twist suddenly, sliding off the side of a root, and it would cause her to nearly fall onto the pile of dirt she was making, and then she would catch herself and want to curse, holding her tongue out of habit. Though in this place who would hear her. She threw her garbage on this dirt in the evenings too, and cut it up with a few thrusts and pushed it down into the clay and remembered she needed to ask Adele where she might find some sand. She would mix this soil and condition it, as she had learned from Zoe, her college roommate, whom she had liked even though she was so unlike Anna, slim and dark haired and short, with perpetually tired eyes and fast speech, who had a huge poster of the Sex Pistols, and who smoked cigarettes and grass, which Anna would not, and who had laughed at Anna's interest in the back to the land movement, which seemed artificial and alien to Anna at the time but now was echoing in her mind and her efforts. Now she seemed to be living the life that Zoe had hated because it was where she came from, her parents old rural hippies. But Anna wanted to discover communities like that and explore what was possible and what must fail because of, well, human nature. So she had done it without quite deciding to at the end of her last term, just driving and looking and thinking and singing to herself until she arrived here, at this river and this house, and wasn't that how we found ourselves, each of us in our own way and time, trying to do something we thought we wanted to do and maybe finding ourselves doing something else, something different, something we thought we might never do, that defines us? At that thought, Anna said out loud, "I won't be defined!" Not yet. Maybe never. It was her primary dread. The only center that seemed to hold for her. She didn't remember when, but this much had come to her recently: every choice cuts off other choices. Every choice shapes us, at least for that time, that moment, that situation; every choice partially defines us until, like a ruthless sculptor scraping away at her block of clay, all that is left is the form, which is now the only form possible because scrape away any more and it may topple or at least will become unbeautiful, and it cannot be pasted back together; slapping handfuls of wet clay here or there won't do it because that too is an ugly act and must create an ugly artifact. It's cheating in fact, and the result will not be a person but something else, like the Golem of Prague she had read about in one of her classes, or some kind of homunculus, deformed and crippled. Where had she heard that word homunculus? The sound of it made her laugh. A small person, a midget. Come to think of it, a tiny baby, a fetus, that was a homunculus. Did that mean it was deformed?

Inside, she lumbered against the counter, holding herself up with one mud-smeared hand while filling the sink and dropping the potatoes she had dug up into the water.

Of course not! Her baby would not be deformed, she had no reason to worry. She stopped, both hands on the counter, shivering now with the coolness of the evening breeze from the open window on her bare shoulders, on her neck, on her bare thighs. How had this chill sneaked up on her so completely? She felt a catch in her throat that she knew would lead to tears, to a brief torrent that she understood she would not be able to avoid, and why should she. Adele was not here, no one was here, she was by herself and she could cry. But each time she cried, she saw those coal dark eyes, her grandmother's eyes, boring into her, demanding she be strong, and the thought of them was more painful than the pain in her throat that came with the tears, and she wanted to stop.

But she couldn't and the tears came and she tried to wipe her eyes with the backs of her hands now, feeling the dried mud still on them, standing up in this excuse for a kitchen and shaking them down toward the muddy water in the sink, shaking them even after the dirt had been flung away and she thrust her hands into the water and rubbed them together harshly, as if in anger. How could she have this baby, she asked herself, how? Alone? But she didn't want the father, whoever that might be, to be here, and why would he come even if she did. That's how she thought of him, "the father," not a man she loved or even cared about. A one night stand, for god's sake, how did she let herself do that? He was barely even a ghost in her mind now. She could do this alone. Frank, who lived in the house next to Adele's, she might have liked his help, lanky and with his own dark eyes, with his worn jeans with holes in the knees, who brought her groceries sometimes and things he thought she might need and who she tolerated but sent away quickly when he came; nor her brother or her sister, both in Hawaii and who couldn't be here anyway, even if she wanted them, nor her father. Her father. When she thought of him, she cried again, with a small cry of anguish because she did want him here, she only told herself she didn't want him because she didn't want anyone, it was just too much to bear having to explain herself or make excuses or be polite or even civil. But of anyone, he would be the one she could talk to. Certainly not her mother.

And then Adele was at her door, knocking and then opening it, and coming in.

"Evening Anna honey. How are you feeling? I saw you come in from digging. I made a pot of that tea you gave me. You want some?"

Anna stirred the potatoes with her hands as if she had been washing them then pulled the plug and let the muddy water drain. "Okay," she said without turning around. She filled the sink again. Then she turned around to face the short woman. "Hi," she said, trying to smile.

"Honey, you don't look so good. Are you sure you don't want me to call your momma?" Adele replied, looking up into her face, setting the pot on the table. Blunt as the stones that bordered her garden, Anna thought. "No, I'm...." and stopped because the pain was like a knife tearing through her middle. She threw one hand to her mouth to try to muffle her scream, and reached sideways with the other to try to find a chair, and missed, and she felt herself falling. As she went down on her bottom she looked up to see Adele pulling her hand out of her coat pocket, holding a cell phone to her ear. The pain was not as intense now, or at least shared out with her butt, which had taken her weight, and her back, which might have hit something on the way down. "Frank?" Adele yelled into the phone, "Get yourself over here. Right away. Anna's house. Bring my station wagon."

WHEN ANNA WOKE, she was in a hospital bed, a tube going into her arm. The pain was replaced by a general sort of ache and tiredness. Frank was reading a newspaper in a chair across the room. The room was plain, not intensive care at least. She was relieved that it was a single. "Hey," she said. It came out softer than she meant it but Frank looked up, stuffed the paper away and came over to her.

"Hey," he said. How you doing?" She stared at him for a moment. She hadn't really let herself look before. Early thirties maybe, skin darkened and lined by too much sun. Hair long, like most of the men and boys who lived near the river, but at least it was combed. A relaxed grin. Caring eyes. It always surprised her, eyes like that, a shade droopy, well spaced, creases radiating from each side, likable eyes, despite what must be a fairly hard scrabble life. Maybe he had kids. Or dogs or something. A caretaker type. So unlike her father's friends at the country club.

"Okay I guess. You tell me."

"I think you started having contractions. Your water broke. Better let the doctor fill you in on the rest."

"Where's Adele? Oh, thanks for bringing me here. I guess."

"She's back home, said to let her know when you woke up. What do you mean you guess? Didn't you want to come to the hospital when it was time?"

She stared around the room. So white. So dead looking, boring, institutional. What did she expect, she asked herself. It's a hospital. "I don't know," she said. "I guess so. I guess I didn't think about it much."

"All right then. No problem. I'm gonna step out and give Adele a call. You get some rest, okay?"

After that she didn't see anybody for a while. Then a nurse walked in and took her temperature and pulse and put on some rubber gloves and squirted lubricant on her fingers and felt way up in her vagina, which she hadn't expected. It didn't hurt but after, she started feeling pulling sensations. Her child was on the move. This was not new, she'd been feeling it for the last few months, but this time it alarmed her, expecting the pulsing pains of labor to return at any moment. "How long between your contractions?" asked the nurse. Anna shook her head. She hadn't felt any since she woke. "Don't know."

The nurse handed her a bed alarm. "Press this when you do feel them again, got it? And the clock is right up there. Note the time. You're doing fine dear. Don't worry. Do you have family coming? There didn't seem to be anybody for you in the waiting room."

"No, no family coming."

The nurse gave her a reassuring smile. "No problem. Don't worry about a thing. You're in good hands here. Dr. Young will be along this evening after supper sometime. He can answer your questions then."

The nurse left, Anna staring at her back. But I don't have any questions, she whispered to herself, except maybe how to get out of here. She looked down at the mound below her breasts. She knew she didn't mean it, she needed help, she would probably die if she were alone, and her baby too, and it would be painful and messy. But if she didn't. If she lived through it, that would be the kind of thing she could remember and tell her grandkids about, wouldn't it. Roughing it on the prairie. A pioneer woman, like her grandmother. Like the women she had read about in American Lit. But she knew she didn't want the pain, couldn't stand it, would run back to a place like this when it got bad. If she could. If she didn't die.

The doctor didn't tell her much. Progressing slowly but that was normal with a first child. They would monitor her through the night to see how her contractions progressed, and decide what to do tomorrow. Did she have any questions? No, no questions, but how long would it all take? We'll see, we'll see, was all he could tell her, then he adjusted something on the drip in her arm and gradually the tension around her chest seemed to relax some, and she turned on the television but ignored it, and stared out the window instead.

WHEN SHE WOKE the next morning, her mother was in the chair by the window. Sallow, tense above sagging jowls, frowning. Staring at her. The last person Anna expected to see. The last person she wanted to see. She wanted to close her eyes and sink back into sleep, or somehow disappear. Her mother rose and walked over to her bedside. "How are you?" she asked in an icy voice.

"Mother...."

"My god Anna. Do you have any idea what you've put us through? For five months now we've been looking for you. We actually hired a detective! He's been checking the morgues all over the east coast. And here you are in nowhere Missouri for God's sake, and about to have a baby! Why did you run away? Why didn't you call us?"

Anna almost smiled. This little speech was just what she needed. It calmed her, condensed her, focused her mind. She had almost panicked when she saw her mother. Now she felt in control.

"Is dad here too, mother? If so, get him for me. Please." She closed her eyes, willing herself to ignore her mother and anything else she might have to say. She heard the stress in her mother's voice, saw it in her face. But it was a trick she had learned: to let it slide around her without touching her. To allow herself to say no to it. At first she felt compelled to argue, to point out to her mother how selfish were her complaints. It only escalated everything, so she finally realized the best way to make it all go away was to ignore it completely. It wasn't easy. It took practice, but she had learned how to find a quiet place in her mind and take refuge there when her mother indulged herself. Her father didn't do this to her, in fact he had helped by pointing out once that her mother was expressing her own pain, was going through "the changes", and that she really had little control over it, and it was up to them to help her if they could, or at least not make it worse. So Anna learned that ignoring her mother when she went off was a good thing, a way to help her mother. At least sometimes she believed that, wanted it to be that way. Other times she just hoped her silence was her own kind of revenge on her mother's cruelty.

Her father was not there, at least not yet. He was flying down and would have to rent a car like she had done last night, her mother said, and should be here later this morning. She said it as if it were bitter news, then stopped talking and walked out of the room.

Anna knew there was little love left between her parents. But at least he was coming. She would talk to him, and maybe her mother would stay out of the room while she did, and then maybe she could decide what to do.

Then her mother returned, and a tall man she didn't know came in behind her, wearing a gray pin-stripe suit and some sort of school tie (she'd seen so many of them on the east coast and they were supposed to mean something, but Anna had never bothered to remember which were which). "Anna, this is Jack. He's a friend of mine. And my attorney." She held out a sheaf of papers at her. "I want you to sign this. It's nothing important but it'll help us move forward. Get our lives on."

Anna frowned at the paper. Her mother snapped the fingers of her other hand and Jack pulled out a pen and laid it in her hand. She thrust the pen toward Anna as well as the paper.

"What is it?"

"Just sign it, Anna. Don't ask questions. You don't have any right to question me. Not after what you've done."

"No."

Her mother grimaced and sighed. She turned around suddenly and thrust the paper and pen into Jack's hands. "You talk to her."

Anna glanced at him. He looked reluctant but obviously had no choice. An employee. One of her mother's servants.

"Hello Miss Hope. I hope you're feeling better." He stepped forward, glancing sideways at Anna's mother, his face taking on a neutral, professional look she had seen before. "Anna, your mother wants you to sign this, but I have to tell you legally you're not required to do so. You're twenty one, age of legal consent in Illinois, where this has to be filed. It's a consent form – a release allowing the state of Illinois to assume responsibility for your child. The child will go to an adaption agency in Chicago, who will find a home for it." He merely held the paper and pen by his side. Anna let out a little sigh of relief. He may be her employee, her attorney, but he was no fool.

"Put it on the table. I'll think about it. I'd like you both to leave please. Send in my dad when he gets here." She turned her eyes away.

The attorney put the paper and pen on the table and turned to the door. "Jack," her mother said sharply, "Jack. You're here to help me with this, and to notarize it. What do you think you're doing?"

"Sorry, Muriel, you can't force her. She's of age." Anna heard his steps fade down the corridor. Anna braced herself, but a few seconds later she heard the clipped sounds of her mother's high heels following him.

It was a slow labor and delivery, a full five days, but successful in the end. Anna's mother stayed the whole time though Anna asked her to leave at least once every day. Her father stayed for two days then had to return to run his business. He called daily, a moment she resented until she actually picked up the phone, then melted almost immediately into her father's smooth voice. She named the baby Alexandria, after her father's middle name, Alexander.

"Your coming home, Anna," her mother said on the last day. "Do you want to pick up anything from that little house you've been staying in?"

Little house, not home. Staying in, not living in. These were like pin pricks or pinches. Deliberate, mean, the sort of small-minded indefensible attacks she had grown up with.

She had talked to her father about this moment. He wanted her to come back to Illinois too. She said she'd think about it. It was an option but not the only one and she really wanted choices. Getting pregnant hadn't been her choice. Or it was in a sense, she realized now. Whatever happened, she hadn't protected herself. Driving west – the only direction she could go. When she reached Illinois she turned southwest instead of north and began to think about how much her life was shaped by others, by their choices, their wills, their needs. She felt unformed, the comparison to a lump of clay was all too obvious to her, she needed to become someone of her own, learn to be the sculptress of her identity and her fate, if such a thing were even possible.

I need to be able to choose this, she had told her father. Now she told her mother, "I'll decide where I go, not you."

"Well of course you will dear," her mother said but Anna could see her cheeks turning red, her neck go straight. Her mother was so predictable, so easy to read. She hoped she might never be that easy to see through. Her mother's plan in a situation like this was, wait for the moment. Wait until she had Anna in her car, then drive her straight to the airport. Anna honestly didn't know if she wanted to return to the little broken down house by the river. She didn't know where she wanted to go. She could go home to Illinois for a few days maybe, while deciding where to escape to. It was a new life, after all, a new beginning, for her and her daughter. But the thought of going back to the huge rambling ultra-modern house on Lake Michigan meant dealing with her mother, every day trying to find her own identity in the face of that pressure. And life there would be comfortable. Way too comfortable. Jack, her mother's lawyer, had left the same day he arrived. He was fed up with her mother too, Anna could tell, but she wished he were here now. He might help her. When her father called that afternoon, she asked her mother for a few minutes alone with him. "Dad, please, I can't come back to Lake Forest. Not right now, maybe later. I need you to talk to mother for me. Tell her I'm not coming back. Tell her to leave without me. I've got the credit cards you gave me. I can take care of myself."

"Listen sweetie. I understand. I think in your place I might want to do the same. But you've got a child to raise now. You're going to need help. I can help you find a place of your own, just come back for a little while and I'll help you get out of here and into a flat somewhere. I'll cover your bills for as long as you need me to, you know that."

"Dad....I don't know. I can't. I just can't. I don't want to come back."

Hearing herself say that brought unexpected tears to her eyes. She blinked and took a deep breath. It seemed like a decision, a real choice. She didn't know how badly she wanted this until she said it out loud. "Dad, I'm not coming back. Not now. Will you tell Mom?"

She could hear her father breathing on the line. Thinking. She'd always been his favorite. His final child and his smart daughter. And it seemed like he always tried to be fair and to give her courage when he could. "That's a big decision, Anna, just you and your girl by yourself. I don't know how you're going to do it. I'll help you of course. With expenses. But about your mother. You've got to stand up to her yourself. If you can't do that, you can't do the rest."

And that was it. So she called Adele. Her neighbor had stuffed her number in Anna's coat pocket before Frank drove her to the hospital, just in case.

"I need your help," she said. "Can you get Frank to pick me up?"

"I thought your parents were with you?" she said.

"They're gone. They've left. I'm coming back. I need a ride. Could you get him to meet me at the front door in about half an hour?"

"I'll try."

Frank called about ten minutes later and it was arranged. Anna finished packing and dressing and walked down the hall to the nurses station, Alexandra tucked in one arm. "I'm checking out. The doctor said I could, right? I'm leaving right away." Then a few steps further to the little sun room at the end of the hallway, painted a cheerful peach and sky blue, with its collection of old National Geographics on a scratched up table. Her mother stood looking out a window.

"Mother, I'm leaving."

"Good. Just wait by the front door and I'll bring the car around. It's about two hours to the airport. You might want to pee first, dear."

"No. Mother, I'm not going with you. Just go on. Please. I'll be fine, I'll talk to you soon. I'm going back to my house. I might find another place later, but for now that's where I'm going to live." She felt herself sweating, breathing hard. Being put on the spot by her teachers at Sarah Lawrence had never felt this hard. She suddenly felt awkward standing there, maybe even a little dizzy. She sat down carefully, holding her baby, checking her face, still red and wrinkled and shrunken looking.

The nurse had said it would change quickly as she fed it. She'd been shown how to breast feed. The nurse said she had good breasts, good milk, that she would be a fast growing, happy child all right.

Her mother stood stiff in front of her. She looked more like the middle school teacher she had once been than the mother who must have once suckled her, Anna thought. Sad and alone here. She looked smaller to Anna suddenly, face collapsed, tears starting. "Anna. That's my granddaughter." Despite everything, Anna felt an urge to go to her and hug her and reassure her. She didn't move.

"You'll see her, mother. I'll come visit. Don't worry. Please, don't worry about us." She stood and turned toward the exit at the end of the hall. She had her baby and one small bag. She wouldn't need any help. The way forward seemed clear to her now. This was all so much easier to do than she had imagined. She started walking forward. I don't know what I'll do after this, she told herself, but I'll do something. I'll figure it out. Her hand on the door, she turned back to the forlorn woman at the end of the corridor.

"Go home, mother. Please just go home."

WHEN FRANK PICKED HER UP at the hospital he asked, "Where to, Anna?" A fair question. But Anna was ready for this one.

"Back to the house where you picked me up." He pulled out silently, a half smile on his lips. He drove to Wolf's Point, turned left past the Wolf's Point hill onto the gravel drive that goes by the shell house Anna was camping in. Just before they got to that house, Frank pulled over and stopped in front of another house, the clapboard house Adele lived in. She immediately came out the door of her screened porch and came round to Anna's side of Frank's pickup. Anna rolled down the window.

"Hi, Adele." Anna held up her bundle. "Meet Alexandria. Alex, this is Adele, your godmother." Adele looked surprised.

"I've never been a godmother," she said. "Am I supposed to do something?"

"No expectations. It's just that I don't know if I would have made it if not for you." Alex scrunched up her little face and blinked.

"Anna, I want to ask you something," Adele said. "Are you sure you don't want to go back to your family? You know things can be a little rough here," she said. "Around the edges, I mean. The river. We never know when it's gonna jump up over the bank and flood us. And most of the people here are great. I mean really great. But every once in a while we get a character or two down here, they wander in and you never know what they'll be like." She stopped, looking embarrassed.

"I'm sure. I've never been so sure about anything," said Anna. "But yeah, I've got some things to figure out too. Like that house. It's not mine, I just dumped myself and my stuff there because I didn't know where else to go, and I may not be able to stay long enough and fix it up."

"And it's no place to raise a child, that house. It's dangerous, all those loose boards and dirt and vermin. Anna, that's what I wanted to ask you: why don't you come live with me? At least until you find a better place? I have an extra bedroom, right next to the bathroom and kitchen. No kids and, you know, since we buried Bill...."

Anna looked past Adele at her house. A neat, well tended little place with flowers all over the front yard and porch. Frank was looking at her too, smiling.

"I ... I don't know. I don't want to be an imposition. With a baby and all."

Frank said, "If you're going to live down here, this is as

good as it gets. Adele's easy to get along with, I can tell you. And she's one hell of a cook. Makes great pies too."

Anna turned back to Adele with a sheepish smile. "Thanks. Thanks so much. Yes, of course. I'd love to." Frank opened his door with a creak and pulled her bags out of the back seat. "Come on in then," Adele said with a bright smile.

Wolf's Point could be described as a classic bounded village with two dozen give or take modest houses plus a church, tucked between the forks of a good-sized creek on the north and south, a massive hill on the west, and an even more massive river on the east. Adele was the image of a modest peasant who has lived here all her life. Peasant is the wrong word, of course, because the archetypal landowner-serf model didn't apply. But imagine a middle-age woman, short and broad in the hips and middle with a round face and a sunny personality. The opposite in almost every way from the women of Anna's home town, Lake Forest, who tend to desperate thinness and seem mostly unhappy while working hard to hide that unhappiness from their friends and, most of all, from themselves.

Adele, on the other hand, was what the youth of Lake Forest would have insultingly called "cheerful," meaning lacking in the kind of damaging self-awareness and irony that automatically turns all sources of joy into its opposite. It seemed to Anna they sought pain in their lives, that it would not be possible to create a persona there unless it was a gloss of shiny pretense on top of wilting hurt.

Anna had seen none of that here, which astonished her at first and forced her to question who she might be, having been raised a hothouse flower of that ultra-wealthy culture. Was it possible she could escaped the fate of the Lake Forest wives? She was no stranger to irony, but could this place have an opposite effect on her? Could it inoculate her somehow against the kind of angst and bitterness she saw in so many of her contemporaries? She intuitively felt the danger of overthinking it. Sometime during her last year at college, she had an epiphany. She had been studying Quantum Consciousness for Dr. Janus's class and at the same time exploring literature related to zen and Buddhism for a comparative religions class. The realization that came to her was that her education — all of her higher education at least — had caused her to reflect endlessly on her experiences. The result was a near-total abstraction of her life. She was no longer able to perceive things directly the way she had when she was a child. Everything was filtered through ideas, preconceptions, expectations. She realized this meant she was comparing almost everything, and everybody, to previous experiences and generalizations about those experiences. She judged things and people automatically. She was encouraged, in fact, to do so by all of her teachers.

What she realized was that, by judging the people around her, she felt judged in return. The result was a low-grade angst that never went away. A kind of mental illness, she realized.

This was a serious epiphany, and she felt it was a true one. It frightened her a bit, and Anna prided herself on being a person who was mostly unafraid of the world and the people around her. She retreated from her classes for a week and huddled, hiding behind her coursebooks while thinking this through. At the end of the week, she could no longer keep this to herself. She found the teacher she most respected, Dr. Janus, in her office. She attempted to explain her dilemma.

Dr. Janus said, "So, you're worrying that your classes have separated your consciousness from the truth of your experiences? That you can no longer experience things directly, is that right?"

"Something like that," said Anna.

"Please, come over here to me, would you?" Anna stepped closer to Dr. Janus, who held out her hand to Anna. Anna took the hand. The moment she did, Janus reached over with her other hand and pinched the back of Anna's hand. Anna jumped a little. "Ow!"

"Okay, sorry. Did you experience that directly, or did you filter it through your mind before experiencing it?"

"Oh!" Anna looked at her hand while she thought about it. "I guess that seemed pretty direct."

"Yes. But I'm not trying to refute your observation about filtered experience. You do filter everything. We all do. But I would like to congratulate you, Anna. You've started to take the next step beyond such filtering. Have you read Freud's *Civilization and its Discontents*?" Anna nodded. "I don't recommend much of Freud's point of view about things, but with that book, he hit the mark. Read some Abe Maslow too – it'll take the bad taste out of your mouth.

"Anna, as I'm sure you know, the process of growing into a fully developed human must involve reflection. Becoming aware of what we're aware of. It's the greatest irony of human consciousness that we are both the watcher and the watched. And of course, it's an endless reflection. We find ourselves aware of being aware of being aware of .... Everything. Out of necessity, we characterize the watcher in ourselves as Self, as an active agent controlling everything. Our decisions. Our actions. Our sense of Self becomes, for most of us most of the time, the all of everything. It's only when we're able to place our consciousness a step above or away from Self, that we begin to experience the world more truthfully, more directly. We might call it a religious experience when that happens.

Many do, and leave it at that. I choose to consider such a step the next true phase of our evolution as individuals. So congratulations to you. You're growing past your old self and into a higher level of awareness. Practice it. It's a skill like any other skill. Encourage it. Play with it. And don't imagine for a moment that you are that higher level of awareness, else you're merely carrying that silly Self along with you on the trip. Self is useful. Self is important. But it's only the servant to the higher truth of experience. So good luck, and happy travels to the true watcher within you!"

Now settled in Adele's bedroom, admiring the buddha face wrapped in blankets on the bed, Anna recalled that conversation with Dr. Janus. *"The true watcher within..."* That phrase rang in her head now louder than ever. Looking at Alex, she felt sure that she, more than Anna herself, was that watcher. A ridiculous notion, of course, but the thought would not leave her. Again and again, Anna had heard the voice in her mind that did not feel like her own voice, her own mind. It was, she was sure, an Other. A mind urging her, helping her, advising her when she reached moments that needed a decision. This child, this perfectly beautiful infant was somehow more than the tabla rasa Anna had come to expect of a newborn. There was, she felt sure, a deep, probably quite old, consciousness in her child already blooming. As she thought this, she watched Alex open her eyes and look up into Anna's eyes. The windows to the soul, so the saying goes. Anna knew these thoughts were so outside the norm that they could signal some kind of mental instability. But she also knew this realization, that her child spoke to her even from her womb, was not a fantasy and not impossible. It was as if Alex spoke. There would be no doubting the truth of it if she did, right? And even if the communication with her baby was silent to the world, even if it was mind-to-mind, it was,

Anna was certain, true and real and necessary. She had left school with this child, had driven to this place (and only this place), knew when she arrived this was exactly where she was meant to be. Exactly where Alex had chosen to be born and to live. Alex her miraculous child. Living here, in what was likely a miraculous place. For what reason, she did not know. But she felt confident that, too, would reveal itself in time.

CHAPTER THREE

Chief Superintendent of Detectives

ON THE THIRD TUESDAY OF MAY, Cameron Sheffield drove his rented Beamer from the flat he had rented when he arrived in Columbia to the Quick Shop just up the road to get some things to start his week: milk for the Earl Gray tea he brought with him from London, and some kind of biscuit or perhaps a bagel, if he could find such a thing. In his old neighborhood in southwest London, it would have been easy to find these things at the bodega barely a block away from his home. Here, in America, nothing was close. Outside of the quite small district the locals called downtown, nothing was within walking distance. One required an auto for even the briefest errand.

It was quite a change from his life and career in London, but a necessary one. Cameron had moved to this place, this spot in the middle of the continent of North America — no, of the United States, as the larger part of North America was north of here, in Canada, where doubtless he would have felt more at home.

But not safe.

He had come here at his daughter's urging. Eve had launched her career with an appointment to the faculty of this state's largest university. Following in her old man's footsteps too, with her Ph.D in Criminology. She had agreed to come over from her home in Cambridge to create a program in the subject. Apparently, silly as it sounds, demand for the subject had blown up in this country, thanks to the many popular programs on their telly that popularized the subject. Cameron tried to imagine dozens, or hundreds, of graduates calling themselves forensic specialists, pouring from that university each year and competing for the few actual jobs in the field. But doubtless, thanks to Eve and her passion for the subject, some of them would excel. On the whole, she said, the profession would grow, as some of her graduates would prove capable researchers. Besides, as she also pointed out, the popularity of the subject would pull many into hard sciences, and in this country, as in Great Britain, that could prove important in the long run, as both nations had fallen behind in technology research internationally.

Quite the big picture thinker, his daughter. It made him proud, her dedication and passion and her successes.

Malcolm, on the other hand. His son by his disastrous first marriage. Not much older than Eve, but so different a person. Equally bright, or so Cameron sometimes thought, but without the focused goal-oriented concentration that set Eve apart. More a poet, driven by his creative impulses. And so angry growing up. He was raised by his mother alone in Manchester after the divorce. A mistake, he felt, but there was little he could do about it. Cameron had rarely seen him while growing up. Malcolm had been sixteen when Mary died. Was it suicide, as the local Met reported? Cameron had his doubts. Malcolm disappeared for months after it happened, appearing repeatedly on Eve's doorstep for nourishment and aid, then disappearing again. Cameron thought it must be drugs, but Eve said no, that Mal was so rebellious that he refused even that subculture.

The day came not long ago when Cameron discovered from a friend in MI5 that the pressure was on to prevent his detectives from investigating a murder that implicated a cousin of the royal family. Cameron immediately ordered a report on the crime. When he found his supervisors reluctant to comply, he quietly took over the investigation himself. It wasn't long before he was ordered to drop it. Not to do so, he was told, could result in "consequences" and the threat extended to his children as well as to himself. It was made quite clear to him that the highest levels of the Met, including the Mayor, wanted him to resign after almost forty years as an officer of Scotland Yard. He would leave his post as one of the highest ranking administrators in the Yard, the Detective Chief Superintendent, responsible for all investigations in Great Britain. But he knew from experience that even that would not suffice. He would have to leave his home, which was hardly even really his home. It was a comfortable set of apartments in a building owned by the Yard and rented to officials like himself.

Cameron had long imagined that, somewhere along the line, he would find and purchase a longboat on the Thames somewhere and spend his final years cruising the canals and cafes along the network of waterways. Retire at the helm of a cozy home on the water.

Now here he was in the United States, hanging his coat in a clean but absolutely bland set of rooms, a transient apartment building in a small city in the middle of the plains of a state named for one of the longest rivers in this continent.

Cameron found milk at the Quick Shop, and also bagels, though they were packaged and tough and came with a small plastic pack of cream cheese. There was no lox though, or any kind of fish. The clerk hadn't even heard of such a thing and reminded Cameron that they were about as far from the ocean as one could get, here in Missouri.

On his way out the door, he spotted a rack with something called the Ad Sheet. Various things for sale. He took one and went back to the clerk. "How much?"

"Free," the young man said. "Anything on those racks by the door are giveaways." Cameron thanked him and returned to his temporary abode. Cameron flipped the pages of the Ad Sheet while he ate his breakfast. It was mostly used cars. In the back were some miscellaneous ads for furniture, exercise equipment and other odds and ends. Then he ran across an ad that caught his eye.

"Live aboard the only genuine paddle wheel river boat on the Missouri River," it said. "Eighty-six feet bow to stern, recently renovated, with a fully reinforced steel hull. Call ...."

Cameron stared at the ad for a moment, trying to imagine what it might be like to live full time on the big river south of Columbia. Then he picked up his phone and dialed the number.

CAMERON SHEFFIELD STOOD ON THE BOW of his soon-to-be new home, his fourteen stone, two meter lean frame leaning against the prow rail that barely reached his knees. This, he allowed, would be more of a precarious business than he had expected. Though what he had expected, he really wasn't sure. Not much, possibly. At age sixty, a retired detective, he had come to this country all too suddenly. There was a lot to get used to. Not having to don his wool suit daily, for example. The odd drawl of the locals where he now lived. Driving the wrong side of the road. And this boat.

"Fay Etta" was her name, blazed in gold leaf relief on her stern. He met with the owner the same day he called, somewhere in the south side of Columbia. After some conversation and examining the specifications carefully, Cameron agreed in principle to buy. But that was not the same as being on her, feeling the hull under his feet and, even docked, the faint motion of the hull responding to moving water beneath it. Also he felt it important to get to know the previous owner. To hear her opinions of the Fay Etta's condition and quirks. The price was quite high, but not beyond Cameron's resources. They drove down together to Able's Landing and continued their conversation on the boat.

"Eighty-six feet, is that right? Would that be at the waterline?" He spoke over his shoulder to Mary Ellis, Anna Maria's owner. She was a slender woman near his age with a narrow face and windblown greying hair, who looked on first glance to be one of those clever but lonely spinsters he was familiar with from his many interviews in London. When Cameron finally met her, he was impressed by her visage. She looked at him more directly than he was used to. Her face was narrow and her eyes sharp as knives as she looked into his. He quickly learned she had a diamond-hard mind tempered by quite a sunny disposition. A barrister ("lawyer", they called them here, Cameron reminded himself) serving the county as prosecuting attorney, a woman of sharp intellect who seemed to see the humor in everything. She had come to own this small floating house with a large paddle wheel on the back when her husband died three years earlier.

"That would not," said Mary. "That would be her overall length. From the rear-most paddle to the end of her shore plank. But I imagine you knew that. A man of your experience and standing would not be buying a boat like this without a thorough understanding of what you're getting into, am I right?"

"You may over-estimate my knowledge of boats, Mrs. Ellis. I am a policeman, land-locked my entire life. Not a nautical man."

"Of course. Well, I'll fill in the blanks then. You need merely ask."

"You lived on her? Then you must know a great deal about how she operates?" Cameron turned and worked his way back toward the cabin door. "Shall we go inside? I'd like a tour of the control deck and engine room. You can enlighten me on what I can expect in the way of maintenance and future repairs."

"I'll do my best. My late husband took care of most of the maintenance, but he kept careful records of all expenses, and a log book with daily entries each time we cruised the river."

They stepped into the lower section, which featured a lounge and dining area, the galley, the head and shower, and behind those, the master bedroom. Mary said, "Please have a seat. I took the liberty of bringing along a bottle of Scotch whiskey from my husband's collection. A single malt, twenty-five years old. Rare, my husband said. I honestly believe he may have treasured this unopened bottle more than me or this boat. After our tour, if you decide to buy, I'll be happy to toast the Anna Maria's new owner."

Cameron looked at the label. The twenty-five year old Macallan. Extraordinary. He'd heard of it but never actually seen a bottle, even in the Mayor's sideboard. As he looked back and forth from the bottle to Mrs. Ellis's hazel eyes, he didn't really need to examine the rest of the boat. He knew this would become his new home.

EVE SHEFFIELD loved her new little yellow and white Mini Cooper. It had enough leg room, just, and barely enough headroom, tall as she was. But the rest of it - just right.

Incredible mileage too, though now Eve could afford whatever she needed. She needed little enough fuel, since her apartment was a short walk from the university where she worked as head of the new Prosecutorial Forensics department. It was Saturday. It had been a busy week, as every week had been for the last year, and Eve knew she should be at her office, small as it was, with its desk and credenza and modest conference table. She should prepare her calendar for the coming week, check assignments and her own teaching schedule, and take new potted plants to replace the ones that had been there all week. Perhaps ferns with daisies and asters this time. She might pick them up at Patricia's. She could just call them and have them delivered, but she loved the blaze of blues and greens and yellows and pinks and the uplifting aromas when she walked into their store. It was a ritual she had begun when she first arrived at her office to find two welcoming gifts, a Garden Paradise gourmet basket with fruit and a bright pink kalanchoe plant, and a bouquet of mixed roses. It all made her feel so welcome. She decided on the spot to bring new flowers weekly for her assistant's desk.

But today was different. She wouldn't go in to work, at least not this morning. Her father, Cameron, had called to say something had come up, something she might be interested in, and he might need her help. This morning she would drive the dozen miles south to the campground where Cameron had his new home on the Missouri River. His riverboat. He had bought it recently from a lawyer friend and she hadn't yet seen it.

About halfway down Providence Road she found a Starbucks and stopped for coffee. She'd had their coffee - it was rather expensive but also quite good. She ordered a cup for her father as well as for herself. She was surprised when she got to the drive-through window. "No charge, ma'am," said the barista

- she had laughed when she first heard the word. It seemed too grand for someone who serves coffee. "The person in the car ahead of you paid for it." Eve could only stare at the young man (quite handsome, she thought, even if no older than most of her students). "Really?" she said. "Why?"

"It happens occasionally," he said.

"Let me pay for the person behind me, then," Eve said with a grin. A fun game, this, she felt. She's never heard of such things in England. She wondered if it was something Americans did. Or maybe just these Midwesterners, who she had found friendly in many ways since she moved here last year.

The last half of the drive grew increasingly beautiful, as the busy urban street devolved to two-lane blacktop and wound through what might be called villages in her home country and into countryside and dense woods. Finally she rounded two tight turns walled by cliffs on her right, and with a final sharp left, she crossed a small bridge over a creek. A hundred meters further was Abel's Landing. She parked just outside the Employees Only sign and walked past the small store with its sign with huge lettering announcing "Bait and Camping", admiring the wide brown ripples of the river to her right. She passed the paved launching ramp, past the store with its open door. Just past a small stage that Cameron said hosted local musicians regularly, she went down stairs to a long dock and the Fay Etta, a paddle-wheel river boat and her father's new home.

Cameron stood at the bow pushing a log away with a long pole. As Eve stepped aboard, he pulled the pole out and stowed it on hooks on the side of the cabin.

"It's good to see you, gal," he said, offering a hand to help her step down from the ramp to the front deck. "It seems I have to call you with something work-related to get you down here.”

“I wish I could just drop everything for a visit, Dad. And I’m sure I will one of these weekends,” Eve said. “You know you sound like your friends down here, now, don’t you? Less like an old Englishman than, what do you call them here, Riverbillies?”

Cameron smiled. “It’s an endearing term, darling. Part of the regional dialect. Come inside. There’s someone I want you to meet.”

Eve leaned into her father and whispered. “You better not be matchmaking, Dad.”

“No such thing. It’s business, darling.” As they stepped down the three steps into the lounge area, Eve saw a large man in a sheriff’s uniform sitting at the kitchen table. He stood when he heard them come in. His head was short of the roof, but just. He nodded at Eve and extended his hand as she approached him.

“Evie, this is Matt Bettman, sheriff of Moniteau County,” said Cameron. “That’s the county right across the river.”

“I know, Dad. I’ve been here for a year now. Hello, Mr. Bettman. Or should I call you Sheriff Bettman?”

“Just Matt, please,” said the tall man. “Glad to meet you. Cameron here has been telling me about you and your work.”

“Why don’t we all sit down,” said Cameron, glancing at how close Matt’s head was to a rafter. “Matt has a case that’s pretty puzzling. And I know how you like puzzles.” As they sat, he continued. “Like I told you, Matt, Eve runs the forensics program at the University up the hill. Why don’t you lay out the case for her like you did for me.” As Matt and Eve sat across from each other, Cameron pulled up a stool and popped the top off the coffee Eve brought him.

“Okay,” said Matt. “Two days ago I was called to the home

of a young man and his sister just north of Prairie Home. The man was dead. His sister was okay but disoriented. According to her, they had been visited by a boy, a teenager we think, maybe sixteen, who came into her house uninvited. She wasn't able to tell us anything useful about the boy except a vague description, but apparently he had done something to her brother resulting in his death. Our medical examiner, Beth Williams, is pretty new to her job. She did her best, but she couldn't determine cause of death. I have her notes and pictures here if you want to take a look."

"I've met Beth," said Eve. "She went through our program last year, as I recall. One of the first ones to take it. She impressed me as bright and competent, a fast learner."

She opened Beth's folder and spread the contents. Matt remained quiet while she looked.

Eve whistled under her breath. "I can see why you felt the need to escalate this," she said. "I've never seen a body so deformed. It's almost like it went under some sort of press that crushed all of its bones."

"That's pretty much what Beth said," said the sheriff. "But that's not possible, given where the body was found. It's an Amish farm. No heavy equipment. Do you think you can help us with this?"

Eve breathed out and looked up. "I don't know if I can give you a cause of death, but I'll tell you this. As a forensic scientist, I'd be a fool to pass up the chance to explore this death. Can I examine the body directly?"

"Of course. Problem is, our budget doesn't make it possible to ship the body anywhere but a local funeral home."

"No problem. My department will pay for transport." She gave Matt her business card. "Have someone from your department call me at work and I'll provide the purchase order information they need." She picked up the folder. "Can I hold onto these?" she said.

"Sure." Matt stood. He looked relieved. He pulled out a small plastic holder and gave Eve his card. "Please, call me or Beth if you have any questions. I really appreciate your help on this." He turned to Cameron. "And thank you for letting me drop in on you. Our state attorney general gave me your name and address and recommended you when I called for help. He said you used to be Chief of Detectives in London? Kind of a big deal? Any chance I might be able to call on you later if we have trouble closing this case?"

"Detective Chief Superintendent, actually. Scotland Yard. Which means I didn't do much field work the last few years. I miss it. So I'll be happy to help. I'm retired now, but I wouldn't mind keeping my hand in, especially on a case like this."

AFTER MATT LEFT, Eve and her father stepped back out on deck. Eve walked around the narrow deck between the cabin and rail, admiring the expanse of the river. The wind was cold, blowing ripples across the water that occasionally broke into small white caps. Eve pulled her coat closed. The trees along the opposite shore were starting to drop their yellow leaves.

"So how do you like it, dad? This boat? Your home? Down here on the river? Will you be able to stay warm enough? You always wanted this, didn't you. You've been here, what, two or three months?"

"Closer to six, Evie."

"Sorry. Guess I've been too busy with my work to pay much attention."

"How's that going, girl? Satisfied you made a good decision to come here? Everything's different, isn't it. Not least, which side of the road you drive on. Feeling good about it?"

"It's all about the work. And that keeps me both distracted and focused, so yes, I still think it was a good thing to come. I have my own department at this huge university, dad. I've been able to design it and set it up from scratch. It means I have to attend endless meetings, especially budget meetings, and schmooze to get support for my plans, but mostly it's been less friction than I expected. They like me, dad. I feel respected here."

"Of course, darling. That's no surprise. I'm happy for you. And proud."

"And you? How do you feel about it all? And that woman? What's her name? Who sold you this boat? You seeing her?"

"Oh Evie. Listen to you. You chide me about matchmaking. We're friends, yes. And I lunch with her occasionally. We've gone out on the river a few times too. Have to, for me to learn how to handle this beast. This place, it's so unlike the gentle flow of the Thames and what I thought life might be like on a longboat there. But I like it. A lot. Yes, as you know, I dreamed about living on the water for decades but that damn job never gave me a moment to think about it, much less make it happen."

"And you're safer here too, right? Away from the politics and pressure of London?"

"That ... don't worry about that, Evie. I'm okay. We're all okay here, best I can tell anyway. The pressure I was getting there, from those folk ... they have no jurisdiction here. Nor do they have any reason to worry about what I might know or find out. That's all over darling."

Chapter Four

A New Home

WHEN RICHARD FORTENOT MENTIONED to a co-worker at his job that he was looking for a new place to move his family, Cal, his boss told him to visit Darwin McMurry at Wolf's Point. "It's a pretty little town, not too far away, and it almost always has an empty house or two. You might luck into a place there." Cal knew the town, more or less, from attending annual parties there in the fall for years. He gave Richard rough directions to Darwin's house. "It's easy to find. Right on the corner of a couple of gravel streets. Ask anyone you find down there, they'll point it out to you."

Richard drove down directly after work that day. Cal was right: it was pretty, even in dry August. Being right next to the river in a valley probably meant fog and mist most mornings, providing moisture. As he drove through it, looking for the house Cal had described, he stopped by a large garden just past a church. He got out of his pickup and walked over to a group of three women who were weeding. "Excuse me," he said. "I'm looking for someone called Darwin McMurry. Can you point me to his place?"

"Of course," said one, a tall woman with auburn hair. She wiped her hands on her apron and pointed. "Just turn left at that first street there and go all the way to the end. It's the white house on the corner."

Richard pulled up in front of the house. Looking up, he saw a thin man with graying hair sitting on a stool, his back to the side of the house next to a door at the top of a long set of stairs. He had a drawing pad and pencil on his lap. Richard got out and stood at the bottom of the stairs. "Looking for Darwin McMurry. Is this his place?"

"It is. Who's asking?"

"My name is Richard Fontenot. I heard he might be the person to ask about places to live down here." The man set down the drawing pad and pencil.

"He might be. I'm Darwin. I was mayor down here, but that was a long time ago. Come on up. I might be able to help." Darwin and Richard chatted for a good while. Finally, when Darwin was satisfied he could trust this young man enough, he advised him to go back and stop at the last house before the Wolf's Point hill. "Ask for Mrs. Richelieu. She's an elder widow who might be willing to rent the top of her house."

AT MIDNIGHT IN THEIR NEW HOME in Wolf's Point, Jess and Tuck couldn't sleep. They each sat on the sleeping pallets Lila had made up for them, their backs to the wall. Temporary beds, she told them. Moving pads Richard had fetched from town plus a sleeping bag and pillow for each. Tuck, a scrawny ten year old, had been the first to sit up, fidgeting. He held the top edge of the sleeping bag in both hands tightly, as if a stiff wind might blow it away at any moment. He rocked back and forth. The old house felt like a ship in a storm to him at that moment.

"I don't like it," he whispered to Jess. "It smells strange in here. Like something old or maybe dead. Can't you smell it?"

"Shhhh," whispered Jess. "Yeah, I do but it's not that bad," he said. "It's just an old place. These pads have a new smell, some kind of chemical. And the sleeping bags are old. Richard got 'em from Salvation Army he said. But Lila said they're clean enough to use."

"I can't sleep," said Tuck.

"Me neither. If we're real quiet, we can just sit here and talk for a while. Maybe we'll get sleepy then." Then Jess had an idea. "Tell you what, Tuck. What would you like it to smell like? I can make it smell any way you like. I know mom said not to make things like that happen, that if I do things like I used to do, it would attract the wrong kind of attention. But it's easy and it's just the two of us here, so I can't imagine any danger."

"What do you mean? What did you used to do?"

"Just little things. I used to make skipping stones out of those big granite stones the Corps of Engineers used for the levee where we used to live. I'd pick one up and hold it in my hand and just imagine it was flat and kind of curved. Then I'd throw it and get lots of skips with it."

"I didn't know you could do that," said Tuck. "Can you show me how to do it?"

"I don't know. I think maybe since we've moved here. This place, Wolf's Point, it's special. Some people, kids anyway, can do things here they couldn't do somewhere else. This place is what some people very long ago called a power spot. I read about it in the encyclopedia mom brought home. This place is where something called 'lay line' come together, or cross each other or something. So people can do things with their minds faster and easier than they could before. Things I've always been able to do but I thought I was the only one. Now, it may be I could help you do them too."

"What else did you used to do that no one else could do?"

"Well, I was able to help us when the weather was bad and things wouldn't grow in our garden. Did I ever show you how to harvest our potatoes? I would just put my hand right down into the earth and pull them out. Mom couldn't do it. She had to use a hand spade and dig them out. And once I changed a chunk of lead that Richard had brought home into something else. Something valuable. I gave it to your pop when he was really mad about Chuckie. It calmed him down. He was able to sell it, I think, for lots of money. Anyway, that wasn't such a good thing to do, I found out later, because when he spent all the money, he came to get more. And I didn't have any lead to turn into gold."

"Okay. I get it," said Tuck. "I remember that part. He was so excited. He moved us, him and me, into a hotel in town and he bought a car. Then he spent all his time at the casino and then he was broke and he came back down drunk. That's when he made me bring him his gun and he was going to go make you ...." Tuck stopped, remembering how he warned Jess and his family, how they all drove away to find safety, how his pop chased them .... Jess put his hand around Tuck's shoulders and held him.

"Shhh, it's okay now," he said. That's all over now. We're in a good place. Doesn't it smell better now?"

Tuck breathed deeply and sighed. "Yes. It smells like when we played in the wildflower field in the spring back home. Oh, I like this!" He was quiet for a few minutes, then he said, "But why did we have to move here?" Tuck asked for the hundredth time.

"You know. Our little house was just too small. You wouldn't want to sleep with me in my little bed there forever, would you? We'd both get cramps and such. Here at least we have a lot more room and we'll have our own beds. And a real toilet with running water. Even a shower! I like that!"

"Yeah, but why did we have to move? Was it what happened to my pop?"

Jess was silent at that. He could barely see the outline of Tuck against the glow of the streetlight shining on the bedroom window. He'd ask Lila to make some kind of curtain for that in the morning. "I think it was not just that we didn't have room down there in mom's cabin. It was that there were too many people wondering about your pop's accident, about us being stuck in the ditch and having to get help to get Richard' truck out, and, you know, your pop's truck down the hillside up against a tree. And then him being there like that. Dead, I mean. Sorry Tuck, I don't like to talk about that, but that's what happened. And Richard explained everything to the police, I think, but he was nervous about being down there after that. I heard him mention a boy who was your pop's friend, Martin somebody, and he worried he might do something bad."

Jess felt deeply sad at having to explain all this to his newly adopted brother.

Tuck said, "I miss Chuckie. And my dog too. You think he'll come back?"

"Your dog? I think we'll see him again, sure," said Jess.

"I mean, Pop was pretty mean to Chuckie and me, he drank way too much. And Chuckie, mostly he was mean too, but at least he was there with me when Pop got going on a binge. So now both of them are gone."

"Now you're with us, right, Tuck? You're safe. Are you glad for that? I am."

"Yeah, I guess I am. Glad you're here at least. I'd be just dead like pop without you I think. What you did ....was that another miracle thing, saving my life, like when you ran out on the river and didn't fall in?"

"Shhhh, let's not talk about that, okay?" said Jess. "We're brothers now. I'll always take care of you best I can, anyway until you feel like you can take care of yourself. When we're a lot older, I'd think."

"I'm eleven pretty soon, right? I'm only two years younger than you. We're gonna be older pretty soon."

Jess said, "Being brothers never changes, it doesn't matter how old we are. Let's try to sleep now, okay Tuck? We got a lot of exploring to do tomorrow. We're in a new place now and Richard said there's good people living here. We'll start meeting them soon. This will be our home, Tuck."

"I don't wanna meet a lot of new people," said Tuck. "I know you and Lila and Richard. That's enough for me."

"Okay, don't fret about it. We'll see what happens soon enough. Sleep now if you can, okay?"

With that, Jess fluffed up the top of his sleeping bag and wiggled his legs down into it, turned over on his right side and messed with his pillow until he was comfortable. After a while, Tuck imitated him and dreams overtook them both.

Tuck and Jess had rarely been out of each other's sight since the move. Tuck liked the little town after being here for a few weeks. He liked that he and Jess could go off to explore the fringes of it. Walking around, looking into all the houses. People seemed nice enough. Walking by the house on the corner opposite their new home, he heard music playing, quiet, pleasant folksy songs mostly. So much nicer than the hokey music his dad, Stevie Ray, used to play on the radio at their old place, really just a small camper, with one bedroom for his dad while he and his brother Chuckie slept on pallets in the living room. Tuck didn't miss that place. The big house they moved into here in Wolf's Point had so much more room. He and Jess could have their own room! He thought he'd like it here all right.

After the thing that happened, Tuck had stayed in Jess's room in Lila's little house. There hadn't been much room there either but he felt safe being with Jess. Really it was a cabin, old and pretty small, but not shabby like the camper their dad brought them to, next to the river and only yards away from Lila and Jess's place too.

It was a month ago, give or take, since the accident that killed Tuck's dad. The image of that moment never quite left Tuck's mind. When his dad ran his old pickup off the road and down a hill, into an oak. There had been a bang, really loud. Tuck had been in the back seat of Richard' pickup with Jess when it happened, Richard and Lila in the front, the truck stuck in a ditch.

They had been trying to get away from Stevie Ray. Tuck knew that much: that his father was raging mad at Richard for some reason and drunk. And had a gun. Tuck didn't know why but he knew his pop and he knew there was real danger.

Stevie Ray must have been chasing Richard, because they had been in a panic to get away from him, and drove so fast that night, jerking this way and that down the blacktop then down a gravel road and a curve too fast they almost slid off, then at the next curve, where they did, and Richard's truck slid its back end around and into the ditch. That's when they saw Stevie Ray's lights behind them coming up fast, and then he must have tried to go around that first curve too fast too, because the lights disappeared and there was that bang as his pop's truck hit a tree.

That part was all a whirl in Tuck's head. It was what followed that wanted to replay in his mind like a bad movie clip. Richard jumping out of his truck and walking up the gravel toward Stevie Ray. Then Jess saying "No!" and jumping out behind him. Then Tuck and Lila. Jess running to catch up to Richard as Tuck's dad limped up to the road toward Richard. His pistol in his hand, the one Tuck had fetched for him at home before he ran out of the tiny camper and up toward Jess's to warn them.

Then that moment: "You killed my boy," said Stevie Ray, slurring and spitting the words, the gun still at his side but swinging up. Tuck knew his pop meant Chuckie, who had drowned the month before while chasing Jess. And the strange thing that Jess did, running out on to the river and not sinking at all, so that Chuckie, mad as a hornet, ran after him, right into the churning water. And never came up.

Richard had stopped just a few feet from Stevie Ray, weaponless, and put his hands up as if to stop what was about to happen, saying "You're not going to hurt my boy," in a clear, calm voice. Stevie Ray, still raising the gun, pointing it toward Jess now. Then the explosion of the gun, and Tuck felt something yank him backward and down and it suddenly hurt when he tried to breath. That was all he could remember. Richard wouldn't talk about what happened after that, but when Tuck opened his eyes again, he felt pain and there was blood on his shirt and Jess had his hand over Tuck's heart and was looking calmly into Tuck's eyes. Then the pain eased and Tuck was able to breath. Stevie Ray, his pop, was sprawled on the ground a few feet away, his body arched over the lip of a culvert, one arm under his head, not moving, half on the gravel, half off, the gun nowhere to be seen, and Lila was weeping in Richard's arms.

The whole thing was like a dream that wouldn't stop looping in Tuck's mind. Afterwards Richard must have called for help, because another pickup came and pulled Richard's truck out of the ditch, and then after a long time some police came and looked at everything and talked with Richard and Lila for a long time and then they went home. To the little cabin on the hill where Jess lived.

From the moment he woke with Jess's hand on his chest, he knew he would only be safe if he stayed close to Jess. He knew somehow Jess had done something to save his life. It took a while, because Jess didn't want to talk about what happened either, but he finally told Tuck that his dad had been angry because of what happened at the river when Tuck's brother, Chuck, chased Jess out onto the jetty and slipped and fell into the river and was drowned. That Stevie Ray blamed Jess for that and was angry about it and wanted to hurt him because of it.

But instead, he had shot at Jess and missed and hit Tuck, who was right behind Jess that night, trying to catch up with him. But Tuck had survived. Don't tell anybody, Jess advised him. It's nobody's business to know what happened, that your dad shot you. He didn't mean to, Jess said. You shouldn't talk about it, he said.

The whole thing was a puzzle though, why that happened or even what exactly happened, because, when Tuck was alone and took off his shirt that night, there was blood, but there was no bullet wound. Not a scratch. And Tuck felt fine, just fine, except for that feeling that wouldn't go away, that he and Jess were brothers and more than brothers now. That Jess had somehow saved his life and he was meant to stay with him, close to him, likely for the rest of his life.

CHAPTER FIVE

Anna Hope

Adele's spare room hadn't been used in ages. Anna had everything she really needed – a bed, room for a crib when she found one, shelves for books and what-nots and a bureau for her clothes. But dusty, so dusty. The air down here must be filled with dust when the wind whips up the sandy soil.

Adele told her the house she camped in, such as it was, was owned by a woman from Texas, a hippie healer who wouldn't have minded her being on her property in any case. There seemed to be a relaxed attitude down here about property generally, possibly because at any moment everything can be washed away by the might of the river moving over this land. It's been flooded many times, Wolf's Point, Adele told her, and it will be flooded again and no one can predict when or how bad. The land here, the houses, are all on a flood plain, only a few feet above the river.

So, Anna reflected, life here is something like a Tibetan mandala: created, and recreated with sand, knowing it will be swept away upon completion. Or like Salinger's story about a fabled sand painting on the beach by Picasso, executed only moments before the approaching tide washes it away. All is temporary, all changes, so Buddhism tells us, and living breathlessly on the edge of immanent destruction has the refreshing effect of focusing the mind.

So much for philosophical rubbish. Time to change a diaper and dust those shelves.

ANNA RETURNED AFTER A SUCCESSFUL shopping trip with all she needed to care for her baby. Most of it came from a sad woman who had equipped her suburban home for her first child, which she lost after nearly a full term. It was a bracing experience but only made Anna more determined to learn what she needed to do to keep Alex safe. After setting up the crib, Anna set out with Alex in a new stroller down the blacktop from Sylvia's toward the river, then right, across a stretch of graveled road over to the next street, also gravel. It was rough going with the stroller until she figured out that the ground on the sides was firm enough to support its wheels. All was silent except for birdsong and a gentle swaying of the sycamores and cottonwoods and feathered pine trees along the way. The street, unnamed like all the streets in Wolf's Point, passed a half dozen quiet clapboard houses, mostly on the right, then a large open yard next to the church, empty except for a large garden. On the opposite side of the street she passed four houses, larger than most of the houses in town. The last one before the high hill out of town was the largest and set back farther than the others. Unlike the others, it had two stories with a small balcony in front of a door on the second floor. The railings of the balcony held what looked like throw rugs, one patterned with browns and yellows, the other with green and orange stripes.

The drive to this house widened to provide parking for two vehicles, one a tan sedan, the other a small Toyota pickup truck. Both were parked at an angle next to a door on the side of the house.

As Anna approached, a man stepped out of the side door and opened the door of the pickup and took out a ball cap. He walked out the drive toward a mailbox. Anna stopped and turned the stroller toward the house as he came toward them.

The man was medium height with caramel colored hair, already blowing in the morning breeze. He looked maybe in his twenties, not much older than Anna. His hands were clean but scarred from hard work. He put the cap on and checked the mailbox. It was empty. Anna smiled and waited for him a few feet away. "Morning," she said quietly. "I'm Anna. How are you this morning?" He stopped and pulled a lopsided smile.

"Mornin'," he said. "Doin' okay I guess. A little worn out from moving in yesterday. This is the first chance I've had to see this place in the early light." He turned around to admire the house. "My name's Richard. Richard Fontenot. We just moved here, like I said. With my lady friend Lila and our boys."

"This is Alex. We're new to Wolf's Point too. We moved here near the end of May. And Alex came along less than a month ago. We're staying down the street with our friend Adele. Do you know her?" She pointed diagonally across the church meadow toward the intersection of the other blacktop and the cross street, at the first house.

"I don't know her, not yet," said Richard. "Maybe I can walk with you for a bit while we talk? I think everyone inside is sleeping late this morning. I just needed to get some air and move my legs."

"Sure. I'm just exploring, actually," Anna said. "I haven't had a chance to walk around and see the town properly yet, so this morning we're just looking around and hopefully meeting some people."

"Same here," said Richard. "Lead on then."

They walked down a lane bordering the village on the side farthest from the river, next to a sharply rising hill covered with brown twisted vines. The lane turned right a short block away. At the intersection, stood a well built, comfortable looking small house with a garden. Behind it, a tool shed and second, larger building that looked like a two-car garage turned into a workshop. The windows were new and weatherproofed. They saw long loops of wool, dyed subtle pastel colors, hanging from a rack.

"Do you know who lives here?" Anna said, guiding the stroller through the smoothest parts of the gravel she could find.

"No idea. Like I said, we just got here, just moved into that old house, the upstairs half of it anyway, yesterday evening. I never had a chance to spend much time up here before that, so...."

"Where are you from then?"

"Me? Or us? My family?"

"Both, I guess."

"Well, we moved up here from a little place near the river maybe five or six miles downstream. Lila's place, it's a small camp shack made into a house. It was just big enough for Lila and her boy Jess when I moved in a couple years ago. Then we had a thing happen and we ended up with another boy, Tuck's his name, so there's the four of us now and we just needed more room. So we looked around and someone said come talk to Ruth Richileau, the woman who owns that house. She's older and lives downstairs and wanted to rent out the upstairs, so we took that."

They turned down the gravel lane toward the river. The next house on the right was silent except for the mewing of a cat in the screened porch facing the street. The house after it appeared empty because of the high grass and bushes around it.

"So where are you from?" said Richard.

"Northern Illinois originally. North of Chicago. But I adopted this place the moment I saw it, and it seems to like me, so far. So I guess I'm calling Wolf's Point my home now."

"What brought you here? Know someone down here then?"

"No. It was ... it was just like it drew me. Or like something in me was telling me where I needed to be. I was driving down the interstate and I crossed the river and after one look, I had to see it up close. This seemed the best place to do that. The rest is, you know, destiny or something," she said, smiling a little.

When they got to the intersection of the blacktop and the cross street, Anna pointed left at Adele's house. "Well, that's where I'm staying, for now anyway, till I can find a place of my own." She stepped around to tuck the blanket securely around Alex and picked her up. "Nice to meet you, Richard. I look forward to meeting the rest of your family before too long."

"Me too. See you around, Anna." With this Richard continued down the blacktop toward Sylvia's house, toward the crumbling remains of a bank, toward the general store and the one- room cinder-block building with the sign, "City Hall", and the river. Anna pulled the stroller through the hedge in front of Adele's and stepped with Alex into their temporary home.

After coffee, Adele said, "I plan to make fresh biscuits and sausage gravy for breakfast this morning, with scrambled eggs and bacon. I know you just took a walk, but this is going to take a while."

"That sounds wonderful, Adele. I think I'll change Alex's diaper and take another short walk. Unless you would like me to help you with something."

"No, dear. You go ahead. It should take maybe forty-five minutes."

The street in front of Adele's is gravel, as most of the

streets in Wolf's Point are. Anna just needed to navigate a few yards to get over to the blacktop leading to the tracks and the river. At first it meant bumping and twisting and shaking and maybe damaging the stroller wheels. Alex didn't appear bothered at all by all the motion. In fact, when she looked at her daughter to see if she was distressed, Anna found Alex awake and smiling up at her. What a child!

She decided they would go over the tracks to see the river, then back to the street that looped opposite Adele's. With luck, there would still be coffee left when they returned.

When they approached the broad parking area next to the river, Anna heard voices. Young voices, probably boys. She continued toward the river, maneuvering the stroller across the tracks and down to the hard dirt beyond.

Two boys sat on the edge of the bank, the massive sheet of water about ten feet below them. Anna didn't want to disturb them, but was curious who they were. Probably not tourist kids, not this early in the morning with no cars parked down here. She began to turn the stroller back toward the tracks when she heard one of the boys say, "Hi!"

Anna turned to look. It was the taller of the two, a sandy haired boy in a cotton checked shirt and bluejeans with knees starting to turn white with wear, walking toward them.

"Hi yourself," she said, smiling. "My name's Anna. I'm pretty new here. What's your name?"

"Jess," he said, coming up to the stroller. The other boy was not far behind him now. "This is Tuck. We just moved here too, last night."

"Last night! Well that's a coincidence. We've only been here a few months. Wolf's Point seems to be exploding all of a sudden."

"Who's this?" said Jess, looking down at the stroller.

"Alex. Alex, meet Jess." To Anna's surprise, Alex made a sound like a chuckle and waved both of her arms as if in greeting. This was about as excited as she'd seen her child get.

"Good. She's finally waking up. I thought all this fresh morning air might help her get moving." Anna bundled Alex's blanket around her and picked her up. She fetched a small bottle of breast milk from the stroller and put the tip in Alex's mouth. The other boy, Tuck, walked up beside Jess and looked at Alex. He raised a finger to tickle her nose.

"Hey baby," he said. "Coochie choochie ...."

"Shhhh," said Jess, and lightly touched Tuck's arm and pulled it back. "Mom says we don't talk to babies like that, babbling and such. Says when you talk to a baby, talk like they might understand what you're saying. That way they learn how to talk better, okay?"

"Okay," said Tuck.

"Actually, recent research indicates babbling to babies may help them learn how to verbalize," Anna said. "Sorry! Here I am babbling on about stuff I know little about. So, who is your mom? Where did you boys move to?"

"A two story house up there," Jess said, pointing. "At the end of the street before the big hill."

"Oh yes. I met your dad. Richard, I think his name is? We had a nice talk." "Not our dad," said Tuck, looking up at me with a bit of a pout. "Not my dad anyways." "Yeah," said Jess. "He is sort of dad to our family though. He's my mom's boyfriend. Tuck and me, we're sort of brothers now, but not by blood. But still." Jess gave Tuck an elbow bump and stepped closer to him. "It's complicated, I guess."

Alex released the bottle and burped, producing a large bubble. Anna took a cloth from the back of the stroller and wiped her mouth. She lifted her arms again and windmilled them more or less in Jess's direction.

"I think Alex likes you," Anna said. Alex was looking directly at Jess, or seemed to be, she couldn't be sure. She had read that it takes a long time before newborns can focus their eyes and distinguish objects from each other. Still, Alex seemed especially focused on Jess, who appeared equally fascinated by Alex.

"I like her too!" said Jess. "I've never seen a real baby before. This one's special. Real special. It's like we're already close friends." Tuck stirred and looked away. He moved a step to one side. But Jess stepped back next to him. "Don't worry, Tuck, you and me, we're *brothers*." Anna put Alex back into the stroller and turned it toward town. "I'm happy to meet you boys," she said. "We both are, it looks like. I've got to get Alex back to Adele's pretty soon – that's where we're staying for now. We're both about ready for breakfast, I think. I hope you boys enjoy your new home. And please stay safe. Adele says a freight train comes through here a few times a day, so it's not a good idea to be close to the tracks then. And that river. She tells me you don't want to fall into that. The undertow, she says. Sucks you right down." She smiled at Jess and Tuck and said, "And that's about all the good advice I've got for you. You look smart enough to take care of yourselves. And each other." Anna gave a little wave as the boys turned to walk up the bank. Exploring, no doubt. That's what she'd do. That's what she expected to do a lot more of as she gets to know this place.

As they bumped their way across the tracks and back up toward Adele's, Anna was struck, not for the first time, by the lush green of this place. Ahead, maples and oaks mixed with feather pines lined all the strects. Behind these, the colors of various houses and vehicles, and like a fine landscape oil, the rise of the hill that bounded this community on the west side, wild with greens and yellows and the twisted masses of grays and browns of the underbrush and fallen trees. And the air: moist but clear and morning cool, so unlike what she had been used to in New York and even Lake Forest.

She looked down at Alex, who seemed to be as amazed by the sight of it all as she was.

CHAPTER SIX

The Children of Wolf's Point

ANNA FIRST MET MARTIN CONRAD at the Spring Party that the town hosted each May. She met a lot of the town on that day. Old and young, they were all friendly and helpful, even chipper, as it was bloom time down by the river. Martin stood out because he was the opposite. Dark hair, uncombed and shaggy, dark clothes. His expression and attitude seemed to say the whole thing, the party, the cheer, was a lie, and that he alone knew the truth about the place and the people in it. Nonetheless, he helped himself liberally to the food and drink that people brought to share.

There was something about him. He was a brooding, unattractive boy and she felt repelled by him. But as she was new to this place, it felt important to her to learn who was who. She was a stranger to the town and she could feel it in the half-smiles and side glances from the people around her. They weren't quick to approach her and say hello but each time she approached someone she found them welcoming and easy to talk with. It was a bit awkward when they asked where she was from. "Illinois," was her usual answer, and "near Chicago" when pressed for details. She knew telling them she was from the wealthy gated community of Lake Forest, Illinois, and, more recently, the even more guarded and artificial environment of upstate New York at Sarah Lawrence, would only embarrass both her and the person she was speaking to. Anywhere else, that answer might have been a brag; here is felt more like the opposite. More than once, she asked people she met about Martin. Of everyone there, he was the only one who made her nervous. He seemed so completely the odd one out, the loner in a crowd. It puzzled her why he was at the party at all. Introverts she understood. She found only the briefest answers. "He got left here when his father skipped out on Sylvia, I hear. She can tell you more," said Chip when she asked. Susie, a cheerful woman in a colorful homemade skirt, selling pies in the City Hall said, "He's dim, bless his heart. Pay no attention to him, honey. But don't leave your purse unguarded, you know what I mean? He's been picked up for stealing in Jamestown a time or two, I hear." Anna learned that he had been a truant and dropout from high school; that his father had built the house on stilts catercorner from Adele's house and was an absent father; and that he was not Sylvia's son. She finally found Sylvia and had a pleasant chat about her work with the town's community garden. But about Martin, she had little to say. "He showed up here with Jack about three years ago while Jack was finishing the house. He's lived with us every since, though he disappears from time to time, probably with his father, I'm guessing. When Jack moved out he left Martin. I didn't really want him here. I'm worried that as my daughter grows up, Martin will turn his attention to her, to put it politely. But I don't think he really has anywhere else he could live."

Over time, Anna was able to piece together more of the story. Jack had left an old farm truck when he moved out. Martin, tall for his age, had the key and though he was only sixteen, he drove it around the county. He had been picked up by the police more than once and had spent some lock-down time in a juvenile detention center. Sheriff's deputies had visited Sylvia, urging her to supervise Martin, but she refused to be responsible for him. He was Jack's boy, and Jack had to take the blame if Martin screwed up.

Everyone who knew him hoped he might straighten himself out, hoped that he might find a way to get along with society and keep himself out of trouble. But it was, by all accounts, faint hope. No one really thought Martin's story would end well.

Despite this, Anna found Wolf's Point a hopeful kind of community. Influenced by the influx of older, educated hippies back in the 60s and 70s, who visited and then moved here, attracted by empty houses and the lush beauty of the place, hoping to form a new, better cooperative and collaborative community. Darwin McMurry may not have been the first to arrive, fresh from his university days, but he was the most influential, the center of a small group of new faces who followed him and settled. Even the locals, descendants of farm families on the highlands surrounding Wolf's Point, after some initial resistance, got to know the new residents with their friendly, broad and inclusive world-views, and adapted to the changing culture that evolved with them.

Jack Conrad was a more recent arrival, with his son. He bought the lot on the corner of two streets, next to an old garage workshop, and set about building a house. He and Martin lived in a small dwelling, a shed really, while he started building the main house. But just after he and his son arrived, Wolf's Point flooded. The water was high, the shed washed away, and when it subsided, Jack decided to build his new house on stilts, sixteen feet above the lot, to avoid being damaged by future floods. Framed, plumbed and sheathed but otherwise unfinished, Jack came home with his new girlfriend, Sylvia, who set about turning the shell into a home.

Martin seemed to like it there for the first few years, but after primary school, found ways to spend less time there. He didn't like middle or high school and would skip it or leave without permission almost every day. The school must have contacted Jack about this, who did nothing to discipline his son. Finally the school threatened to expel Martin. Jack, who hadn't finished high school himself, ignored this too. His attitude was "it's what he wants, right? I can't help him. He'll get the education he needs the hard way, like I did." He made Martin come home at least some of the time so he could make him go with him to jobs pushing dirt. He gave Martin a few bucks on these occasions, if Martin was useful, but never as much as it would cost him to hire real help. For Jack, Martin was little more than cheap labor.

Anna learned most of this from Darwin in conversations over coffee in the mornings. His friend Mel O'Dell was there too, in and out while doing chores and working on his projects. "He may be a bad seed," he said once. Darwin jumped on this. "No such thing, I'd think," Darwin responded. "We can't know, and we shouldn't judge." Mel winced at this. "Quite right. It was hasty and ill thought. The jury will please disregard the comment," he said, winking with a grin. "A carnation short of a bouquet though, if you ask me."

A fleeting shadow of worry passed through Anna when she thought about Martin. She planned to raise Alex in this otherwise friendly community. What if Martin turned out to be a threat? Then she realized this was unlikely, as Martin would be grown and long gone by the time Alex was a teen. Besides, it wouldn't be possible to protect her from all dangers. The best Anna could do would be to help her learn how to protect herself.

Alice Johannson walked along the railroad track toward the steel bridge over the creek. She walked carefully, stepping the long steps between the ties, examining the plants that grew between them and to the sides of the steel rails. What she really hoped to find was a special kind of mushroom: *Amanita Muscaria*, the one with bright red caps with white spots. It wasn't for eating, that one. She knew it would make her sick. Sylvia had refused to teach her mushrooms. Not yet, she said. Someday, when she was older. But this one she knew from her books on witchcraft. It was about the only one that she could identify clearly, in fact. She recalled the picture in her mind: the stately, firm, colorful little thing that looked like it might have been created in a Disney cartoon and transplanted to this world. She held the image as long as she could, then opened her eyes and looked, to the left, toward the reeds bordering the bank of the river. And there it was! Just as if she had made it appear by thinking about it. Pleased, she stepped over to it and pulled the plastic bag from her back pocket. From inside it, she pulled out a paper towel and reached down carefully, her fingers protected by the towel, and broke the mushroom from its stem and put it in the bag. It was smaller than she thought it might be, but she had no doubt that this species could protect itself. Thus her caution.

It was a small victory, but it was the only one. She continued walking, peering along the bank as she went. There were no more mushrooms of any kind to be found.

After about half an hour, well down the tracks into the

wooded area south of the creek, she finally turned back. As she walked back, continually scanning the bank for more *Amanita* but expecting none, since she'd looked as carefully as she could going down, she decided to try something. She stopped, closed her eyes, and again pictured the brightly colored, deadly cap in her mind's eye. Again, she held it as long as she could. Then she opened her eyes and looked hard at the bank. Nothing. So she continued her walk. What a silly idea, she thought. That thinking about the mushroom, picturing it in her mind, might magically make it appear. But how would she know if she could ever be a witch unless she experimented? She took another step, looking at the bank, and .... There! Larger than the first, sunshine reflecting from its red and white cap.

Just as if thinking about it had made it appear.

Maybe it does work, almost holding her breath at the thought. Maybe it just takes a little while to appear.

She continued her walk toward home. She stopped periodically, pictured the mushroom as clearly and as long as possible, then opened her eyes and continued walking.

Before she reached home, she had six of the colorful caps in her bag. She went up the stairs and into the house. She was burning to tell Sylvia about this, but no one was there. Sylvia was out at the big garden. Alice went into her room, closed the door, and opened her books. Could this be how one learned to be a witch? She could find no mention of the technique. In fact, she found no mention of witches making things magically appear at all. It might have been something sorcerers could do, an entirely different level of magic altogether. Alice's mind was spinning. She realized she should say nothing about this, at least to her mother or other grownups. But there was one person she could ask. She took her bag of mushrooms and left, determined to find and ask her new friend, Jess.

ALICE DIDN'T KNOW Jess well. She'd only met him recently but she liked him immediately. She decided this ability, or whatever it might turn out to be, was too important to wait, so she walked up the street toward the hill and the house Jess and his family had moved into. Along the way, she saw him and his brother walking down toward her.

"Hey Jess," she said as she reached them. She turned back to walk next to them. "Can I ask you something? It's something odd. It's never happened to me before, I think. It's like I can imagine a mushroom and it appears. Or I think it does, it could be some kind of coincidence I guess. But I was able to do it over and over." Jess stopped walking and turned toward Alice.

"Yeah?" he said. "Tell me more."

"Well, I was walking down the track this morning, looking for these." She held up her bag of Fly Amanita.

"Those are poisonous, you know," he said. "Don't eat 'em. They'll make you real sick."

"I know. I wasn't going to eat them. Anyway, I couldn't find any, until I did this thing. I pictured it in my mind. Then when I looked up, there it was. Like it just suddenly appeared. I thought it must be, you know, a coincidence. But then I tried it again and it worked! Another one was just there, where I'm pretty sure there wasn't one before. I did it six times in a row!"

"Okay," said Jess. "You're sure you never did it before?" "Pretty sure. Or if so, I wasn't doing it deliberately. Maybe I did and just didn't notice?"

"Yeah," said Jess. "That could be." Tuck was standing next to Jess, looking hard at Alice.

"Naw, that c'aint be true," he said. "Ain't no one can do that. Make things just appear with their mind." He looked up at his brother, puzzled and a little angry.

"Well I did so!" said Alice. "I did it over and over," she

said, making a face at Tuck.

"Wait Tuck," said Jess. "It could be she did do it. See, I know it's possible. I do it all the time when I need to find something. Remember I told you about the things I can do that other people can't?"

"Yeah, okay, but how? I don't see how that's even something anyone should be able to do. It's got to be a trick."

"Take that back!" said Alice.

Jess took Tuck's hand and said, "Shush now, both of you. Just let yourself think about it like it's possible and you just never noticed it before. I know it's possible, Tuck. I expect you've been doing it too, without knowing it. Lots of people have."

"That's silly," said Tuck, but quieter. He was much calmer now that Jess was speaking to him.

"How come I've never heard about it before?" said Alice.

"Probably because it just seems natural, like you said, like it was a coincidence."

Alice said, "Do you think we should tell the grownups? Sylvia? Or your mom?" Jess looked thoughtful.

"No. I don't think they'd believe us. It might even make them worry. See, the thing is, they can't do it. Not like you and I can. Or maybe they can, but it happens so slowly for them that they don't believe they're doing it with their minds. We can do it better and faster, because we're kids. The younger you are, the better you can do it. I'm pretty sure that's just how it is."

"Can I do it too?" asked Tuck. "Like with money? If I imagine I'm going to find like a penny or something? Then it'll just appear?"

Jess said, "Maybe. But it's easier and faster with natural things, like those mushrooms. Doing it with made things, that's slower and harder. You might have to try over and over and over and still it might not work. And the thing is, trying to do it is harder than if you just accidentally do it. And if you do it to make yourself rich or to hurt someone, it probably won't work at all. Or if it does, then you'll pay a price for that later. Doing it to help someone other than yourself, that might work, though I can't help thinking even that's risky. It's like there are rules for magic or whatever we want to call it. We've all got this ability, I think. I think we've always had it too. But something changed and now it's all much faster. It's this place too, this village. We kids can do it much faster and easier here, like Alice's mushrooms."

The three continued to walk slowly toward the river together, lost in thought.

After a while, Alice said, "What happened, I wonder? You said something changed, right? What could it be? Do you mean just to us? Or everybody?"

"Everybody, I think," said Jess. "I don't know exactly what happened, but I think it was gradual, like over a lot of years. Imagine the whole world was bombarded with an invisible ray that kept us from being able to use our minds, and then the ray went away. And because it's left our minds quieter now, we can begin to do things we were always meant to be able to do."

WHEN ALICE RETURNED home with her bag of *Amanita* mushrooms, she was burning to tell someone about her discovery. When she reached the deck of her house, Martin was sitting on the bench, cleaning the mud from under his fingernails. As usual, he looked unhappy. Alice decided to reveal her new powers to him. "Look!" she said, holding up the webbed bag proudly. Martin merely glanced at her and grunted. Then he looked again at the brightly colored red caps.

"What's those?"

"Mushrooms. They're poisonous. I found 'em. Lots of

'em."

"Lemme see," said Martin. He took the bag from her and opened the top. He lifted out two large ones and held them up to the light.

"You better not be gonna eat those, Martin." Alice reached for the ones Martin had taken out of the bag. He cupped his hand in front of them and moved them away from her.

"Poisonous? You sure? I'm keeping these. You got plenty there."

Alice grabbed the bag and held it behind her back. She rarely talked to Martin. At sixteen, he seemed so much older. And he mostly ignored Alice. She knew Martin had a mean streak, so she was usually careful around him. But she had done something special, making these mushrooms appear. It was something she could do and he couldn't. She couldn't resist bragging.

"I made 'em appear," she said with a huff. "I made 'em all just pop up so's I could pick 'em."

"What you talkin' 'bout? Made 'em appear? You found 'em, that's all."

"No I didn't! I pictured 'em in my mind and there they were. Over and over until I had a bag full of 'em!"

"You found 'em. I think you better leave me be." "No, it's true! I can show you, if you want to see." "Show me what? How bat-shit crazy you are?" "C'mon down with me. Watch me make more of 'em appear," Alice said, turning back to the stairs. She had nearly reached the bottom before she heard Martin start down the stairs above her.

They walked north beside the tracks, Martin trailing Alice by a few steps, watching her. She felt she had best explain, so he would understand what she was doing.

She walked past the clearing to the undergrowth a few feet

from the tracks. Alice said, "Okay now. Look up the side there, at all those reeds and bushes? See any mushrooms there? See, there aren't any, right? Now, I'm gonna close my eyes and picture a red speckled mushroom in my mind." She stopped and silently closed her eyes. Martin watched the brush where she had pointed. Suddenly he saw it. A bright spot of red low to the ground. He grunted. Alice opened her eyes and scanned until she saw it.

"There. Did you see it appear?"

"Naw," Martin said. "I see it though. I just had to look hard enough to spot it. It was already there."

Alice turned around and scowled. "It wasn't there. You didn't just find it. I told ya, I made it appear." She could see the confusion and doubt cloud Martin's face. She walked to the mushroom and plucked it into her bag. "Let's walk back the way we came. No mushrooms, right? We already walked by all that. Now watch me while I make another one appear where there ain't any." She started walking ahead of him. Reluctantly, Martin followed her, this time watching the grass and brush to the left carefully as he went. After only a few steps, he stopped suddenly. There it was, unmistakably bright red and white, growing at the edge of the grass where he was sure there had been nothing but grass and sand and gravel.

"Okay," he said. "How'd you do that?"

Alice felt a thrill run through her at his words. She had done it, convinced her hard-headed brother. It verified her power to her in an entirely new way.

As they walked back toward the crossing and their house, Alice did her best to explain how she manifested the mushrooms. She told Martin what Jess had said about her powers, how she was just getting started with her skills, how witching (as she liked to think of it) was a new thing that certain people could do if they applied themselves to it. How maybe even he might be able to do some of it, though she would have preferred to think she alone had such abilities. "Don't tell mom about this. Please, don't tell anyone! Jess said I shouldn't talk about it."

Martin was burning with curiosity. His imagination was wild with the possibilities. He determined to try Alice's method himself. Not with mushrooms but with something. "Yeah, don't worry, I won't say anything about it."

After Alice's demonstration with mushrooms, Martin returned to his room and took down a ceramic bowl given to him by Sylvia in which he kept small things he wanted to keep. Nail clippers, a class ring he had found in the sand by the tracks, some unused fire crackers. He found what he was looking for: a pair of dice. These he had picked up from a table in the bar in Jamestown where his father went after jobs. Not old enough to sit at the bar with Jack and the rowdy crew of mechanics and farmers who practically lived in the place, Martin plunked himself down in the back at a table with magazines. The table was square with recessed pockets on each of its four sides. One of the pockets held the dice. Martin sat on the end of his bed now and threw them several times. He began thinking, if he could throw sevens, or deuces or elevens, and do it predictably, that would mean he had powers like Alice. Useful powers at that, better than making stupid mushrooms appear.

Nothing happened. He threw the dice repeatedly for close to an hour but, best he could tell, they always came up random. The longer he tried, the more angry he became. "Not fair," he hissed to himself. He tried drawing a pair of dice faces on a piece of paper and watching it while he threw. No joy.

When he got tired of throwing random numbers, he stopped

and wondered if he was doing it wrong. Alice, that stupid bitch, hadn't been throwing dice. She had made mushrooms appear, magically, out of nowhere. That was because she wanted more than anything to become a witch. He'd heard her tell that to Sylvia.

She said she pictured the mushroom in her mind and then it appeared. Right, well, there was something he wanted more than anything else too. He rifled through his magazines until he found the picture he wanted: a color closeup of a Beretta 9-millimeter pistol. He stared at it then closed his eyes and tried to hold that picture in his mind. He wished it to appear in front of him, right there on his bed.

Nothing.

He tried three times but each time he opened his eyes to see nothing but his crumpled and stained sheets. After the third try, Martin was so angry at himself that he yanked up the dice from his desk and squeezed them as hard as he could and threw them against his bedroom wall.

Except what came out of his hand wasn't dice. It was a handful of dice, small as grains of sand. They scattered over his bed when they hit the wall.

He laughed with surprise. Eyes wide, a grin spreading, he picked up one of the tiny grains and looked as closely as he could. Squinting, he could tell it was something like a die: a distorted, bent cube and dots so small he saw them only as smudges. But he could see the grain was six-sided, as dice were. He examined two or three others, all slightly different from one another, all distorted cubes.

He gathered them all, or all that he could find given how chaotic his sheets and spread were, and put them together in an empty Coke bottle.

He felt a glow growing in his stomach. It didn't hurt – it

made him want to laugh. He had a secret! Something no one else, he was sure, could do: change things with his mind.

He put the bottle on a shelf where he could admire it when he want to. After a minute or so, he glanced at it and surprise again: it looked different. Peering through the wavey green glass, he saw that the tiny bits of the dice had clumped together into a lumpy, very distorted single mass randomly splattered with dots. Hundreds of sand-grain sized bits of dark plastic had become a single blob.

He shook it: it was solid, all right. It rattled about inside the bottle like a trapped critter of some sort. Martin laughed again. He realized there was no way he could have gotten that thing, whatever it was now, through the narrow neck of the bottle. It felt even more like a prize now. He put the bottle in prize position, between the shell of a large bore rifle cartridge, and a shotgun shell, still sealed and potent, with the brass bottom scratched from laying for years among the stones between the tracks north of the town creek. The bottle and its contents had an even greater aura of potential than the treasured ammunition.

FOR THE FIRST TIME in his life, Martin Conrad felt driven to learn a new skill. He was overwhelmed by curiosity. Those dice! He had changed them somehow, though he didn't really know how and he hadn't meant to change them into ... whatever they became. Since that moment, Martin had practiced. He tried changing the dice again, over and over. He wasn't able to break them apart as before, but they did change, usually to flattened or twisted versions of themselves. He soon discovered something else: they changed back within a few minutes by themselves. He didn't will it or even think about it ... they just reverted to their original shape. So it seemed this skill, changing the shape of things, must be temporary, at least at this stage. At first, Martin thought he had to hold the dice, or whatever he was trying to change. Then he discovered that he could make them change by just looking at them and forming a picture in his mind of how he wanted them to change. Nothing worked until he thought to try a small change, like their color. He started with a white sock. After a few tries, he succeeded in changing its color to a light orange. Successive tries resulted in darker colors until finally he reached a deep red. Then when he tried to change the mating sock, he was thrilled to find it changed immediately to the same color. He worried that Sylvia would notice and ask embarrassing questions, but as he watched, the socks reverted back to white.

Satisfied with this, he concentrated on changing the shape of an object. As before, he had to take baby steps until he achieved his goal. He tried to bend a pencil, but only a little. On the next try, the pencil snapped in half. So, he figured, wood, or things that are brittle, must have limits, regardless of magic. He took out a metal shirt hanger and put it on his bed. He pictured it bending in some way. There was no immediate change until he pictured only part of it changing: the long straight part at the bottom. He imagined it curving up like a bow being pulled. It instantly obeyed. Martin was thrilled. He picked it up and admired the curve. It seemed to vibrate in his hand. As he held it, the curve disappeared. The hanger returned to its original shape.

With practice, he managed to twist the entire hanger into a complicated knot which lasted about two minutes before it slowly unwound and untwisted back to its original shape.

Martin was disappointed that his magic didn't last long, but otherwise he felt a power growing in him that he had never felt before. Each time, the feeling fed a hunger he didn't know he had. He wasn't sure when, or if, he would reveal his abilities to anyone else, but if he did, he realized, he would command respect in a way no one could deny. This was an irresistible thought. But who could he reveal himself to? Perhaps, he thought, it didn't matter who. No one could deny him anything now. He could ask for anything, demand anything, and if he met resistance, he could overcome it now, with his mind. It was a superpower. He gasped with the realization that he could not be denied what he wanted now. But he knew instinctively he must be careful. He must practice and master these abilities. Find out how far they extend, how much he could actually do, before he revealed himself to anyone.

Looking for ways to try his new powers, Martin walked up the street toward the hill. When he got to the second from last house on the left, where a older woman named Susan lived, he noticed her car was gone. She lived alone and raised most of her own food there. She even had a small greenhouse. Martin went in. The planting beds were empty. Mid-summer was just too hot to grow things. He walked through and out the rear door. There was a garden filled with mostly brown stalks of sunflower and corn. Next to it was an enclosure, fenced in with chicken wire, where he found rabbits huddled near their feeder. She must harvest them for food, thought Martin. He wondered if she had to chase them to catch one so she could chop its head off and skin it. Behind the enclosure he saw rabbit skins stretched out on sheets of plywood and next to that, a large stump with a hatchet embedded in it. Then it occurred to him. What a lot of trouble to have to capture one. If they could do what he could do .... he decided to try it. He focused on one of the rabbits, white with chocolate spots and a black patch covering part of its face. First he concentrated on changing the color of the patch. Quickly, it changed from black to light brown. The rabbit seemed unaware of the change. After about two minutes, it changed back to its original color.

Then Martin took the next step. It took him a moment to figure out in what ways to change its shape. Then he had it. He held the image in his mind while watching the rabbit. It flipped on its back and squealed as its legs stretched out in four directions. It seemed to grow larger as it flattened to resemble the shape of the stretched skins Martin had observed. As it did, he heard crackling and a gurgling sound and watched as blood spew from its mouth.

He stopped with that and waited for it to resume its original shape. After two minutes, the rabbit started to shrink back to its original shape and size. But the transformation seemed to stop before reaching its original size. The rabbit lay on its back with no signs of life.

Martin felt a bit horrified by what he had done as he walked away from the pen and back to the front of the house. But the feeling faded and was replaced by a secret satisfaction at his abilities. This, he realized, was real power. The power over life and death.

CHAPTER SEVEN

The Woman with No Past

THERE WAS A MOMENT IN THE MORNINGS when Ruth Richileau was able to feel free and happy. Sometime after rising, most often with the sun, after washing her face and arms and emptying her bladder, and just sitting there in her bathroom, looking up at the little window above the shower. It was then she was able to imagine, at 90 years old, what it was like to be twenty again, with Charlie, her new husband, in the next room getting into his overalls and boots, almost ready to go out to work, when he would say softly to her, "Good morning my lovely lady. Are you going to have another fine day here in paradise?" and she would reply, "Yes my love, we will. But you come back to me safe, you hear?" and he would reply, "Yes'm, I hear and comply. 'Cause I will always come back to you!" and then she would hear the bedroom door close and she would know he was gone.

It was a good moment, that memory, as long as she was able to delay remembering the day he did not return, the day that man from the factory came to her door with the pastor of their church behind him, neither of them smiling, not there to ask her to bake a dessert for the church. Ruth did her best not to remember that moment, but she always did, it was the biggest and most painful memory in her box of memories, and it would not be contained for long.

But now the moment was past, and Ruth – Mrs. R to these new folk she chose to help by sharing her big old house – made her way from the bathroom, through the bedroom, pulling up the covers of her bed just a bit as she went, out through the hallway to the kitchen and sat back down. Her breath was short these days, she didn't know how many more she would have, but she thought not many, and it gladdened her heart when the woman of the family she rented to came down the steep stairs from their apartment and into the kitchen to make them both coffee, she with cream, Lila without.

A curious woman, this Lila, Ruth thought. But a good one. Quiet, modest, thin and not tall but strong of body and quick of mind, anticipating Ruth's needs without asking, doing what she could for her, though it was no part of their bargain to live here. She seemed just to want to help and to spend time with Ruth, and Ruth was grateful for that. It had been so long and she had been alone for too many years in this house, making do, stepping down the porch steps to walk to the mailbox or the church across the street and to visit her friends, all of whom were gone now. Her legs, her balance, her strength, were almost gone too. And she had no interest in church anymore. All that seemed like a different age for her, a different time when she was a different person. She still read everything she could get hold of though, still curious about everything, and now Lila helped her with that too.

She tried not to spend a lot of time thinking about the past though. It would be foolish, she felt, a weakness that would lead to something she didn't want – insanity maybe, or senility, which she was pretty sure she had avoided. And that was a miracle, she supposed, at her age. She felt clear of mind and clear in her purpose: to help these folk upstairs, to help their boy, whom she knew was special in some way. To end her days calmly and as placidly as possible.

And the boy, Jess, was helping her with that. She didn't know how it might be possible, but there it was: he visited her, he spent time with her, and it was as if he were young Charlie, as if he could somehow inhabit him while with her. Quietly, oh so quietly too; as if speaking directly into her mind. It wasn't memories, exactly. It was Jess, she knew. It wasn't an illusion. Jess seemed to know exactly what to say, what to do to comfort her and let her relax into herself.

THE DAY HAD STARTED NORMALLY ENOUGH for Lila. They had only been here a month but already she felt herself settling into comfortable rituals. Wake with the sun, so much brighter here first thing in the morning than it had been down in the valley in her old house. Make coffee and a small lunch for Richard to take with him to his job as a farm hand for Mr. Carter. Make sure the boys were up and wearing clean clothes, then fix them breakfast. She didn't have to worry about Jess. He could take care of himself and always had. But Tuck sometimes didn't know what to put on and was groggy and unsure of himself first thing in the morning, so she made sure he had clean jeans and socks and a tee shirt. Then wait until she heard Mrs. R come out of her room, then make coffee and sit down and chat with her until she tired and returned to her room. Then clean and tidy the house.

This morning was the same until Mrs. R came out of her room to the kitchen. It was like her speech and movements were all in slow motion, like some part of the aging woman was lingering behind her body.

"Oh Lila, I'm so tired today," she said. "I don't know if I have the energy to do anything but nap. Maybe I'll knit some later, or maybe read. Those are relaxing enough. I don't know what's happening. You don't suppose I'm getting old, do you?" she said looking up at Lila with a weak grin.

"No, Mrs. R. Not a bit of it," said Lila.

"Well I am though, and I don't know how much longer I can carry on here. I just need someone. Someone I can count on. To be here." Ruth was taking quick breaths between sentences, which made Lila clutch her coffee cup all the tighter.

"I have something I need to ask you," said Ruth, breathing hard. "Can I count on you?"

"Yes, of course you can," said Lila. "What do you need, Mrs. R?"

"I need you to take care of that boy of yours. Oh, I know you will, I know you're doing that now. That's fine. But I want to help," she said. "I want to help," she repeated, looking down now at her hands. "I need to ask you if you would take the place when I'm gone, to care for your boys. Do with it whatever you like. You could sell it if you feel the need. But it isn't worth a lot, I think. That man Jack Conrad said he wants to buy it but he wouldn't pay much for it and he's gone I think.

"Besides, I don't want to sell it. To anyone. I've been here for over seventy years. I want you to have it. And your man, and those kids. I'll gift it to you. Will you let me do that? Accept it?" She looked up at Lila, her eyes brimming. Lila stared back at the old woman across the table, whom she had known for only weeks.

She cared for her. It was easy to care for her, she felt. What was she to do? Would it be right to accept an offer like that?

"I .... I don't know what to say. Mrs. R, we love you. Please don't talk that way. I'll help you. We'll help you, any way we can. Please don't talk about dying!"

"Lila, hush. I don't have any family. No one to come watch vigil, no one to inherit. My Charlie and me, we tried but we couldn't have children. Then he died, so so young. And the factory, they came and said how sorry they were and all, and then they gave me a check. They tried to make it all okay by paying for the accident that killed my husband. So I took that money and bought this house and I've lived here alone for such a long time. And now it's time to pass along the fruit of that blood money. Please Lila. Let me give you the house. You've got those two boys to look after, and ...."

She paused and seemed to struggle to take a breath. Lila said, "What is it, Mrs. R?"

"That boy of yours. Jess. Lila, do you know how special he is? He comes and spends time with me in the evenings. Every evening since you all came here! He sits with me and .... I don't know how to describe it. While he's with me I feel young again and back with my Charlie and all my worries, they just dissolve. He's a wonder, that boy. A treasure. He seems to glow! It's really him I want to give the house to. To Jess. Because what he's given me since you came is worth more than gold, worth more than land. I can't tell you how happy he's made me, your Jess."

Lila looked down at her hands in her lap, blinking. "That's fine. I'm glad he makes you feel better. Thank you for telling me."

Ruth put her handkerchief to her eyes and nose and looked up at Lila. "Honey, I have a question. You don't have to answer. Is Richard the father to Jess? He's a good man, surely he is. But there's something about the way he acts around you, around Jess especially."

"No m'am. He came to us about two years ago, from down south somewhere. I was living alone with Jess."

"I know I'm prying," said Ruth. "But I'm an old woman. Who is Jess's father? Is he special too, like Jess?"

"Mrs. R, Ruth, I wish I could tell you. The truth is, I just don't know." Ruth smiled and dropped her eyes. "Oh, it's not like that," said Lila. "I just don't remember. Anything from that time. Something happened, I don't know what, but everything before Jess was born is just a blank for me. It's like I was born at the same time he was. Like we both woke to the world at the same time. Does that make sense? I don't remember anything about who I was then, how I came to the place where Jess was born. My name, I had that, but that was it. I was alone, there was nobody with me when he slid out of me. It was so strange to open my eyes and there he was, this baby on a blanket, both of us stark naked. I knew enough to bring him to my breast, to find some cord and a knife and cut the cord, and get us both cleaned up and warm. Honestly, I don't know much more than that. We were alone in a motel room. I had clothes and some money and even a car. Once I knew we were okay, I took us out and we drove north till we found a little house abandoned next to the river. It was the river that drew us," Lila said, nodding toward the river edging Wolf's Point. "I don't know how we got by but we did," she said. It wasn't that hard for some reason. We had shelter and food just seemed to come to us when we needed it. Jess was an easy boy to raise, it didn't matter that I didn't know what I was doing. We lived that way for close to ten years until Richard came. We fell in love with him right away and he with us, and not much changed except he was a hard worker so we had even more, and he taught Jess all he could, though Jess could already read and such." Lila looked stricken. "Oh, Mrs R, I haven't told this much before, to anyone! Not even to Richard!"

Ruth leaned forward the took Lila in her arms. "Lila, honey, don't worry, I won't be telling your story to anyone, I promise! You poor girl! What could have happened to you to cause you to lose your memory like that? It must have been something terrible, I think!"

RICHARD CAME HOME from work that night, more tired and restless than usual. It had been a hard day, harder than most because his boss, Cal, had been particularly demanding and ill-tempered. Richard understood why Cal was that way – there were plenty of pressures on him, and then one of his calves had disappeared and Richard had ridden out to find it in the four-wheeler and then had to walk down a wash to a creek where he found it dead. All while the work at Cal's slaughterhouse was stacking up because one of his other men had failed to show up for work.

Anyway, it was always something.

Richard was determined not to unload his day onto Lila though. They had moved into Mrs. R's house not quite a month ago and doubtless Lila had her hands full too, taking care of Jess and Tuck. And Mrs. R, too, from what Lila had told him. Lila seemed to welcome this chore but it must be getting harder. Mrs. R was failing, Lila had told him. Dying.

It was sad news for them, of course. Mrs. R had been good to them, surprisingly good, actually. When they first knocked on her door and introduced themselves, about four weeks ago, the town's old mayor, Darwin, was with them. Mrs. R knew Darwin well enough, which made introductions easy. Darwin explained that Richard and Lila lived down Fox Hollow Road by the river, over near Jamestown, and they needed to find a place to live with more room, since they had just adopted a boy about their son's age.

Ruth had smiled and invited them in for coffee and asked them to tell her their story.

As Darwin had expected, the timing was right. He knew Ruth, though active and independent, was slowing down and probably needed help with things. The upper half of her old house was furnished but empty and Ruth never went up those stairs anymore. She agreed almost immediately to let the family move in, especially if Lila could help her with chores and cooking and such. They could talk about rent later, she said. For now, she just needed some help and maybe some company occasionally. Lila and Richard went upstairs to look around while Darwin caught up with Ruth in her kitchen. Richard started moving the family in the next day.

Since then, Mrs. R had still not mentioned rent. Richard wondered about that but didn't worry about it. He had some money saved. Besides, he told Lila, it was a country thing, to share and to barter and to avoid the formality of contracts and such whenever possible. It had been how things were done down where Richard came from, and it was true up here in Missouri as well. A man's word was everything out in the country, everyone understood it and tried hard to live up to it. About the worst thing a man could do with his neighbors was make an agreement and then fail to live up to it.

Richard felt much better after a shower and change of clothes. But he couldn't help worrying. If Mrs. R died, would they have to move out? Just as they were finally getting settled?

He and Lila sat in lawn chairs outside the side door of the house, enjoying the evening air and waiting for the boys to return from their day's adventures. That's when Lila told him about Mrs. R's offer.

"Oh it makes me so sad," Lila said. "She's dying. She says she feels like she won't live much longer." She lowered her voice and said, "Richard, she wants to give us the house! She means it. She says she's already called a lawyer friend to come out and help her sign it over to us. She says she doesn't have any family to give it to, that we're the closest she has now to family. Oh Richard, it's so sad!"

Richard didn't know what to say, it was so hard to take it in. "You mean, the house? The whole house? We wouldn't have to pay ... anything?"

"I think so. That's what she was saying. Just free and clear. Property taxes once a year but in Wolf's Point that doesn't come to much money. I'm sure we could handle that. She said she liked us so much, with me helping out every day, and you too, but she said she's especially fond of Jess. She said she really meant to help Jess if she could. He's been spending time with her at night, before she goes to bed I guess. I didn't know about it, and you know, it's got to be okay .... she just loves Jess so much, she told me. He makes her feel young, he takes her pain away somehow. Something like that. And we know Jess could do something like that."

"But we told Jess. We told him he must not do any of his miracles here, do anything to get him noticed. It's dangerous, Lila, I feel it. Do I need to talk to him again?"

"I think it's okay. I think he knows what he can't do safely. But this ... Richard, how could it be wrong, or not good, or dangerous? He's been comforting her. Making her final days as easy as possible. And it's working, I can see it in her face every day. Richard, she's not in pain, even during the day. She smiled every time I see her. And when Jess is in the house, she has a special look, soft and easy and welcoming. He's helping her, Richard. We can't interfere with that, we just can't."

Richard couldn't help feeling conflicted. Of course they would accept the house. He felt grateful, but also a little guilty for feeling good about the death of their landlady. The thing was, it was the second time in only a few months that someone's death had solved their problems. But this time it was none of their doing.

"No, we can't interfere with that, Lila. I'll thank Mrs. R for her generosity. For being so good to us here."

After her conversation with Lila about the house, Ruth called her lawyer and asked him to come see her. Then she wandered room to room with a small notebook and pen and wrote down a list of some of her favorite possessions. She thought it might be a longer list than it was, but over the years she had gifted one family or another with things they needed, or she felt they might need. It had been her hobby years back, to go to yard and estate sales, pay as little as possible for one thing or another, bring them home and stuff them into her house or the small garage, and then find people who needed them and give them away. She remembered the times Charlie would go with her. He would smile and stay silent as she bid on things at auctions, and drove her to yard sale after yard sale and find room in the trunk of their car or the back seat for another rocking chair or child's high chair or a set of china she just loved or yet one more cast iron skillet. He was good to her that way. He never complained. He might say something like "can't afford that one, honey," once in a while, and she had appreciated that, since he earned their money and had a better idea what's what when it came to what they could afford.

The most expensive and useful things she put on her list were the dining room table, made of solid maple that she and Charlie had bought at auction, and the walnut bureau by the wall next to it, broad and deep with enough drawers to hold two big boxes of silverware and two sets of china plates and saucers. On top, on yellowing hand-wrought doilies sat matching sets of bowels. This was perhaps Ruth's most valued possession, this bureau. Her mother had given it to her when she married and moved into this house. Her mother had been gifted it by her mother too, so it must go back to the late nineteenth century. Ruth wrote "bureau" on her list and underlined it. It was one of many things she had treasured far too long. It was time to mentally turn them all loose.

When she couldn't find anything else to put on her list, she went to the kitchen, took a sharp knife from the dish rack where Lila had put it after washing, picked up the firmest tomato she could find from the bowl on the table, and sliced it into four pieces on the cutting board. She shook some salt on each slice and slid it into her mouth, savoring the succulence and flavors. Her lunch eaten, she lit a burner on the stove, held a corner of the list she'd torn from the notebook in the fire, and dropped the flaming piece of paper into the sink. She watched it devour itself with fire and breathed a satisfied sigh.

That night, she felt what seemed like a new kind of tiredness. It started as sluggishness in her legs and arms, and then in her chest. When Lila came into her room to ask if she wanted to join them for supper, she said, "No, honey. Not tonight." Nor did she eat anything after that for three days. She was able to get herself to her bathroom and back, just, but mostly stayed propped up in her bed, her books and magazines spread around her.

The third day, she asked Jess to come sit with her.

She wasn't in pain except for the discomfort of lying in bed. Lila had been turning her on her side and rubbing salve on her skin to soften it. This helped, but her buttocks and legs and shoulders were sore all the time now. Except when Jess came.

That evening, when Jess came to her after supper, he said, "Hi Ruthie. Can I close the door? We could talk or I could read to you if you like."

"Yes, please do close the door, Jess. I'd like to talk, just the two of us."

Jess pulled the chair up close to her and held her hand. Ruth stared at him. She was afraid to say what she saw. First it was the soft yellow glow surrounding him. It was as if Jess were bathed in a light all its own. She realized suddenly that all of her pain and ache were gone. She felt like she were floating. There was no pressure, just the feeling of being caressed gently.

"You called me Ruthie," she said, smiling at Jess. "No one's called me that since Charlie died."

Jess closed his eyes and nodded.

She looked more closely at him. He didn't look like a boy at this moment. "Are you an angel?" Her expression at that moment was direct, frank, inquiring. She meant it literally.

"Do you want me to be an angel?" said Jess.

"I think you must be. You look like one to me. I never thought an angel, my guardian angel, would be so young looking."

"No younger than you are, Ruthie." And it was true, she knew he was right. She was young. As young as when she met the boy she would soon marry.

As she looked at him, it seemed to her that he was that boy. "Charlie!" she sighed.

"Yes," he said. But he wasn't the boy she had met any longer. As he stood up, she realized he was the young man she had married when she was eighteen. He leaned down and kissed her lips.

"Charlie, what's happening? Are you here? I'm so happy to see you!"

"I'm happy to see you too, Ruthie. Shall we skedaddle out of here? Go have some fun together?"

"Oh yes, Charlie, yes. Please take me out, won't you?"

"All right. Come on then." And she did. She swung her legs over the side and stood in Charlie's arms. She was wearing her wedding dress and Charlie had on the suit he had borrowed from his best friend. Arms around one another, they stepped out into the garden behind her parent's house where they were met by the flowers, the many many flowers her mother had always grown and that she had arranged into bouquets to celebrate their union.

CHAPTER EIGHT

Anna Hope - The Move

IT WAS THE PURR OF FRANK'S BOAT that woke Anna from a troubled dream. All she could remember was trying to free her legs from deep mud while trying to cross a stream, struggling to stay upright while worrying she would pull her feet out of her expensive new boots. She wasn't worried about her pants, an equally expensive pair of Calvin Klein's, because they had been more or less forced on her by her mother when she was leaving for summer camp. Then, the stream, or was it a lake? And she had to get across because the rest of her tent- mates had gone in a canoe ahead of her and she was late, and then at some point she got stuck in that mud, and looking down, she wasn't even sure she had put her clothes on at all, so the Calvin Kleins didn't matter after all.

Anyway, that was as much as she could remember. She pulled the covers aside and swung her legs over. They felt tired, even sore, so yeah, she must have been slogging it out right there in bed, in her head.

She got up as quietly as she could and stepped over to

Alex's crib. Still asleep, breathing normally. It puzzled her, how could she have such a peaceful kid when she herself was anything but. Like a counterbalance in a centrifuge, or kids on a see-saw. Maybe too quiet, too, what's the word, quiescent? She should ask a pediatrician sometime. Not take everything for granted, not assume Alex is okay just because she's to easy to care for.

Not that she minded; Adele had told her stories about colic babies, about how they howl all night and no one gets any rest, maybe for a year or more. Adele rushed to assure her it would be okay if Alex turned out to be like that, that Adele would help, the whole town would do whatever it could to help, and please don't worry about it just because it could happen. Adele couldn't help herself, Anna thought at the time: she just has to voice the worst possible scenario as if to ward it off somehow, and it seemed to work in this case. Here was the quietest and most beatific baby she'd ever seen, Adele said, beaming down at the child in her arms. No, she hadn't had any children, she said, repeating herself needlessly, but that too was okay with Anna: it was Adele being Adele, and the best Anna could do was accept her, be grateful for her help, not judge her, certainly. Not judge anyone. It was an idea she had learned in a psychology course when they were reading the works of contemporary philosophers. Was it Ram Dass? Or maybe that teacher from California who led a bus load of hippies east and then settled in, where? Tennessee, she thought. The Farm. Stephen Gaskin, that was his name. The biggest lesson she had learned from his writing, the most radical, was that we could choose to be angry or not angry, or to judge others or not, that being reactive was a *choice*. That anger was self- indulgent. Growing up, she had always thought the opposite, that people did things to annoy or frustrate or hurt us, and we had no choice but to react to that with anger and disgust and judgment. But Stephen was telling his commune and the world that we could control that, that we can control ourselves and be better people *if we choose to*. A truly radical idea.

So she was trying to practice that. Testing the thesis, at least. Practicing calmness. Maybe that was something she had passed along to her daughter in some mysterious way? She had read somewhere that meditation had that effect: that it somehow affects the genes so that what one struggled to achieve becomes easier, even natural and part of oneself. If so, wasn't it possible to pass those genes along to a child? Affect future generations? True or not, it was a wonderfully hopeful idea, that the human race could, perhaps gradually, over many generations, become better, smarter, more adjusted to the pressures of modern life, of overpopulation even. That our thoughts are under our control and affect who we become, how we live, and all that has the potential to spread like a virus.

All these morning thoughts! Wake up, girl. Get dressed, get out into the world, this new world you're in. Learn who's who and what's what. That, too, is a survival practice, isn't it? Adaptability. Maybe that's why she was down here at the end of a long road, at a place that stops because the river takes over and one has to cope.

WHEN ANNA WOKE FROM HER LATE MORNING NAP, Alex was awake too, waving her arms and making soft sounds like a dove cooing. "Good morning my lovely. Hungry again already, are we?" Anna picked up her baby and sat with her back to a pillow against the wall behind her bed. She lifted her night shirt and put Alex on her left nipple. Alex took three sips of her breakfast and pulled away, her arms back up in the air. "So, not that hungry? Okay." She pulled open the back of Alex's diaper. "No mess, but wet. You're getting pickier, darling. Let's get you changed.”

While changing Alex’s diaper, she heard a soft knock on the bedroom door. “Adele? Come on in.”

“Good morning Anna,” Adele said. She looked sad. “I have fresh coffee out here. Would you like to come out when you’re done?”

Adele did this, Anna had learned, when she wanted to talk about something. “Sure,” she said. “I’ll be there in a flash.” She carried Alex, in a fresh diaper, out to the kitchen. Alex was making ‘*mmm-mmm*’ sounds with pursed lips, which Anna knew meant Alex was ready for more of her momma’s milk. Anna sat and turned partially away from Adele, who was in the chair opposite. A courtesy, though Adele had said she didn’t mind the sight of Anna’s bulbous breasts. “I hope you don’t mind. It looks like Alex may be ready for her morning meal.”

“No, of course not. Go right ahead, honey.”

Her girl now in place and hungrily sucking, Anna said, “So, what’s new, Adele? Anything going on? I heard the phone ring this morning.”

“Well, yes. I had a call from Susie, who lives next to Ruth Richileau, in the big white house just before you go out of town. She said Ruth passed away last night. Ruth wasn’t well, I know that. It wasn’t cancer or anything like that, I don’t think. I think she just got so old she couldn’t keep going on.”

“I’m sorry to hear it, Adele. How old was she?”

“Over ninety, I think. She was a sweet person. I haven’t seen her for several years now, but she was always good. Very generous. She gave me that towel rack next to the stove. She was always finding things for people. So I guess we’ll have a service for her in the church across the street from her house pretty soon, seeing as how she didn’t have family to take her away. They may bury her in the churchyard too, I’m not sure.

The church has room for a cemetery, but it's never really been used that way. Ground's too soft to put coffins in or something like that.

"But honey, there's something else happened. Ruth, like I said, didn't have anyone to pass her property along to. And she apparently just fell in love with that new family that moved in there recently. Susie said Ruth told her their boy was something special. Jess his name is. She really cared for him, I guess, because Ruth gave that family her house!"

Adele paused for a breath and a sip of coffee, looking over the top of her cup at Anna.

"Anna, you might want to go over there and talk to those folk. I mean, you're more than welcome to stay here, you know that. But if you're thinking you need more room, or more privacy or something, they might rent you part of that place. It's pretty big as I recall. And the upstairs was turned into an apartment with a kitchen and bathroom and its own entrance. "I wanted to let you know, just in case you're interested!" she finished, with a big grin.

Anna took the hint. The last couple of weeks she and Adele both had been kept awake by Alex, who was becoming more verbal with her demands for attention in the middle of the night. More than once, Anna had come out to the kitchen after changing her diaper to find Adele there, looking bleary and sheepish, asking if there were anything she needed. It wasn't a big deal, but it would likely be over time. More privacy could be a good thing for both of them.

AFTER LUNCH, ANNA PUT ALEX in her stroller and took a walk to see the river. It was cooler than normal for July, else she wouldn't have gone out mid-day, but it was, she thought, kind of a perfect day. When she crossed the railroad tracks and pushed out onto the flattened earth leading up to the bank of the river, she found Chip untying the rope to his boat. There was no dock. There were wooden stairs leading down into the river, with iron rods pounded into the ground next to every third stair on both sides. Each secured a cable across the back of the stair, holding it firmly to the bank. Chip's boat was tied to one of those. Anna watched as he removed the rope to his boat from one of these anchors and move it up to the next higher one. "Morning!" she said when he finished.

"Oh, hi Anna. How are you today?"

"Fine. You're Chip, right? Darwin's brother? We met at the spring party."

"Yup, that's me. How are you getting along? Adele treating you well?" he asked, climbing up the ladder to the bank above.

"She's been an amazing friend. I don't know what I would have done without her. And Frank. They both took care of me when I was having my baby." Chip looked into the stroller and smiled.

"She's a pretty baby all right. Looks like you. I guess. I don't know babies. Last one we had was close to thirty years ago now."

"So what are you doing? Moving your boat?"

"Moving it up. Or getting it ready to move up when the river rises." Chip looked out and sighed. "It's starting to come up, I'm afraid. So I'll likely have to come down here every day, maybe every few hours if it rises fast enough, and move that painter up a notch. If I don't, and it gets high enough, it'll pull my boat right under."

"So the river's rising? It doesn't look much higher than it was last time I looked. Yesterday," said Anna. "Why do you think it's going to rise?"

"Well, I check the prediction for it every day when I have my boat in. There's a web site that tells high high it is and what the Corps of Engineers thinks will happen over the next week or so. They say it's going to rise pretty fast starting probably tonight."

"Why," Anna said. "It's been dry here, so what makes it go up suddenly?"

"A couple of things. There's been a pattern of heavy rain up north and to the west, in Nebraska and north Missouri, for one thing. That raises the level of the creeks and rivers that feed the Missouri. It just takes a while before we see all that water. It can come up pretty fast when it starts rising. And also, the river way up stream, in the Dakotas, that feeds into dams and when it gets too high, the Corps will dump it to take pressure off the dams. So that water adds to the river coming up from the rain." Chip walked back to the top of his stairs and looked down. "I just hope it doesn't get too high or I'll have to pull my boat out. That's a lot of trouble, but there it is. Life on the river." He turned back, gave Anna a wry grin, and tromped over to his car, shedding mud from his boots with every step.

RICHARD TAPPED LIGHTLY on Adele's screen door. It was late morning on a Saturday. He didn't see anybody through the kitchen window. When there was no response, he opened the door quietly and stepped onto the porch and knocked on the kitchen door, a bit more firmly. Anna came out of her room and opened the door. "Hi Richard. Won't you come in?" "Thanks Anna. How are you doing? How's Alex?"

"We're fine. She's growing really fast, I can tell you. Would you like some coffee? I can reheat some for you." She was speaking quietly. "Adele's sleeping. I think she's not feeling good this morning. Did you want to talk to her?"

"To you, actually," said Richard. "Sure, I'll have a cup if you don't mind. No need to reheat it though. I drink it cold all the time, especially up at the farm." Where he worked, Anna understood. She plugged Adele's old coffee pot into the wall anyway.

"So, how are you doing? And Lila and the boys?"

"Everyone is fine, now that Mrs. R's funeral is over and all the paperwork signed for the house. Anna, it's the house I wanted to talk to you about. Wanted to ask you if you might be interested in moving in there with us? There's so much room there now and, you know, it's quiet. A bit too quiet for Lila anyway. She used to spend her mornings chatting and helping Mrs. R, and now I go to work and .... I think she's lonely."

"I think I'd like that," said Anna, pouring hot water into a tea pot and stirring in some honey. "Tell me more about the place"

"Well, as you know, as everyone in town knows, she gave it to us. She was incredibly generous, that old lady. We all miss her a lot."

"I didn't know her very well. Not at all, really. I've never been in your house." "You should come on over first chance. Here's what we're thinking. We live on the second floor, have right from the start. She had the first floor. Naturally, she didn't want to use the stairs if she didn't have to. But we don't want to move downstairs. We're all settled in up there, and there's enough rooms for Jess and Tuck to each have their own. So that's nice. Downstairs, there's just one bedroom plus the living room and big dining room and kitchen. And bathrooms on both floors, so there's privacy and such. We'd like to rent out the bottom floor, to you in particular, if you'd take it. The rent wouldn't be a lot. Really just enough to help us cover taxes and utilities. Say, a hundred a month maybe? Or we could, you know, work something out ...."

"That's more than reasonable. Money's no problem for me. My family's helping me. I'd love to see it, but I think you can consider it a done deal. But why me? Why do you want me to live there in particular?”

“Well, we thought you might want more room. You know, more of a place of your own. We wouldn’t disturb you very much. Even the boys, I think. They were pretty good about that with Mrs. R and I think they’d respect you the same way. Especially Jess. Actually, Jess is the one who suggested we ask you. Truth is, Anna, he really wants you to live there with us. He won’t say why, but we think he’s just really taken with little Alex. Funny, isn’t it, a kid his age.”

“How old is he?” “Twelve. Getting close to thirteen.” “Well, that’s great. I really like Jess too. I like Tuck too, but he seems harder to get to know. Is he really Jess’s brother? He’s so different from him, from you all, I mean.” Anna looked down and busied herself pouring herself a mug of tea. She face was red. “Sorry, that’s pretty personal, isn’t it.”

“It’s okay,” said Richard. “We adopted him. There was an accident. A couple of accidents, actually, and he lost all his family. He was already close friends with Jess, and we just ... oh, we felt we wanted to take care of him. It’s a long story. But yeah, he’s a little moody, but basically he’s fine. Jess watches out for him. They’re almost never apart, those boys.”

Anna looked up and smiled at Richard. “Okay then. Thanks for asking me. The timing is pretty good, really. Adele has been so kind to us but I think she’d like to have her place back to herself at some point. I’d like to come up and take a look, maybe later today when Alex is awake?” Richard stood up, finished his coffee and offered Anna his hand. “Anytime. I’m home all day today and Lila is there. See you later then.” He let himself out, closing both doors quietly, so not to disturb Adele. Anna got up too and looked out the window over the sink as she washed the cups. She hadn’t gone outside yet, but she could tell it was another beautiful day in Wolf's Point.

As she dried them, she heard the swish-swish of Adele's slippers on the linoleum floor behind her. "Can I fix you anything, Adele?"

"No thanks honey. I just got up to take my antihistamine pill. It's this mid-summer pollen. I've always had allergies, and this is the worst time of year for me. This and late fall. I don't know why. It's the goldenrod, I imagine. I heard you talking to someone. Who was here?"

Anna felt the teapot. It was still pretty hot so she poured a cup for Adele. "Here you are. I'll get your pill if you like. Sit down and drink this. It's got local honey in it. I've read that if you drink it often enough, it'll help you develop an immunity to whatever pollen was gathered by the bees that made it."

"Oh honey, that sound like an old wives tale to me. But thanks, I'll have it anyway."

Anna went to the bathroom and found Adele's bottle of antihistamines. When she returned with it in her hand, she said, "Adele, I've got some news. I hope you're okay with it. It was Richard I was talking to. He and Lila have invited me to move into Ruth's house. They want to rent me the bottom half where she was living." She watched Adele for her reaction. Adele blinked and looked up at Anna with a smile.

"Why honey, that's terrific news. You'll have so much more room, and probably more privacy, don't ya think?"

"I told him I was interested. I'm going over to take a look after I've fed and changed Alex."

"Well that's just fine," said Adele. "I'll miss you being here, of course, but not so much I'd want you to pass up an opportunity like that."

"Thanks Adele. You've been so kind to me. To us. You know you can count on me for anything you need, anytime.

And we won't be strangers. In fact, I may have to ask you to keep an eye on my little one sometimes while she grows up."

"Oh, I hope so. I'll be aunt Adele to that child until I die. It's been a privilege to be part of your lives. So, yeah, I hope you'll be happy there. I hope you two never leave our little community, Anna."

THE MOVE WAS ASTONISHINGLY SIMPLE and quick, from Anna's point of view. She hadn't accumulated much since arriving in Wolf's Point, and had brought little more than a basic wardrobe with her when she arrived. Frank handled everything and wouldn't let her lift anything other than Alex. It all went into the back of his little pickup truck. In minutes, he had unloaded it all into the white house at the bottom of the Wolf's Point hill. Lila announced she wanted to prepare a welcoming supper for everyone involved, including Adele. Baked trout with a homemade sauce, a fresh salad made from the community garden with chunks of pears and walnuts, cornbread baked with sharp cheddar chunks, fresh green beans with almond slivers and for dessert, crumble cake with peach slices and, for the boys, apple pie and ice cream. Since Anna had done little else other than make up her bed with her own sheets and the quilt made by her grandmother, she insisted Lila let her help prepare the meal. "I need the experience," she said, "and I've been looking forward to getting to know you better."

Lila responded with a hug. "Me too," she said.

They chatted as they worked. Much of it was Anna getting to know where things were in the kitchen, and some of their personal histories. Anna was intrigued to learn that Lila remembered only the last dozen years of her life and nothing earlier than that. It was a puzzle that she wanted to explore, how a person could forget so completely and for so long, but she held herself back from pressing Lila. She did hear the stories Lila had to tell about their recent history. How she had lived alone with Jess, raising him in a little cabin near the river for close to ten years; how Richard had appeared in their lives and they fell in love and how he had been a fine, reliable helpmate and tutor to Jess, teaching him to write. Then the harrowing story that culminated in the move to Wolf's Point: how Tuck's brother chased Jess out onto the jetty and fell in and was swept away; how Tuck's father, Stevie Ray, had gotten drunk and chased the family, trying to kill Jess; how he recklessly shot at Jess and hit his son, Tuck; how it appeared that shocked him so much that he died of a heart attack and she and Richard kept Tuck after that. How Tuck wouldn't leave Jess's side, convinced Jess had somehow saved his life. She told this story in a low voice, nearly whispering, and asked Anna not to repeat it. That the story was sad enough and raised so many questions that she and Richard felt they could protect the boys best by avoiding the rumors that they had somehow killed Tuck's father deliberately.

"What a strange story," said Anna. "I'm so glad you shared it. I won't repeat it, I promise."

Lila looked close to tears. "I just needed to tell someone. I feel like I can trust you. It's been such a burden. Not that having Tuck has been a burden, not at all," she said brightly. "He's a good boy and a good friend to Jess. And Jess .... I always worried that he would be alone all his life. Jess is .... you'll find out, I think, ... he's special. Very special. I don't know who his father is. It's all a blank before Jess came along. But he can do things. Things that no one else can do." Lila sniffed and reached out to squeeze Anna's hand. "I've said too much, I think. I've never told anyone but Richard all this stuff, and here I am, unloading on you and I've only just met you. You're easy to talk to, Anna. Thanks for that. Now, let's get this meal started!" She found one of Ruth's aprons and handed it to Anna. "Maybe you can help me figure out what order to fix things in so it all comes out together?"

CHAPTER NINE

Magic Spins Out of Control

LELAND DAHL WORKED THE NIGHT SHIFT at the little Quick Shop store over on the west side of Jamestown. He was a single fellow, lanky and a bit shaky after not enough sleep. It was never enough sleep with him, had been all his life, it seemed. His remedy was bennies and small nips of Southern Comfort to get through the night. He was only an hour into tonight's shift when he had to pee. He looked to see if anyone was in the store he hadn't noticed, but the place was empty. There wouldn't be this time of night on a Tuesday. He turned the key that locked the register and stepped out the back of the sales enclosure and over to the bathroom.

"Shit," he said to himself when he finished peeing and looked at himself in the mirror. His loose brown hair was all over the place. He had forgotten to comb before he left for work. He didn't particularly care how he looked but his boss would if he showed up, which he did three or four times a month on different days of the week. Sneaky bastard. Leland stepped out of the bathroom and over to the miscellaneous goods rack. There was a comb there, he kind of remembered putting out a box of them last week. He found one and went back to the bathroom and tugged the comb through his springy tufts. It reminded him of when he borrowed that brush cutter from Ray down the road to cut the long weeds in the ditch beside his mother's house. His hair was tough like that tall grass and hogweed and nettles. Back out to the counter. No one in the store but there was someone with an old pickup out by pump 3. He couldn't see him very well but didn't need to. Those pumps were all self-serve, which meant he didn't have to do anything unless someone wanted to pay by cash.

He watched as the guy, a kid with dark hair wearing a worn out plaid over-shirt, pulled the hose over and put the nozzle into the fill hole and squeezed the handle. He watched the kid for a while. There wasn't anything else to do right now. The kid looked frustrated. Angry. Pretty soon he came around the pump and started toward the door to the store. He looked mad about something. Leland braced himself.

There was the familiar creak and buzz when the kid opened the door. He marched up to the counter and stared hard at Leland. "What'ja need?" said Leland.

"I can't get your pump to work," said the kid. "I tried everything. I was gonna pump me ten bucks worth and then come in and pay you."

"Don't work that way. Sir. You got to pay first and I turn on the pump for that amount." "Well, I was gonna pay after. Go ahead and turn the pump on." "Sure," said Leland. "Ten dollar's worth, right?" The kid turned and went back out to the pump. "Hey! No money, no gas!" Leland shouted after him but the door had already closed. He watched as the kid went back to his truck and squeezed the handle to the hose a few times. Then he almost ran back to the store.

"Yeah," said Leland. "You forgot to give me the ten bucks first."

The kid stared at him, hard. "Naw, I don't have no ten bucks. I just want you to turn on that pump so'z I can get gas."

That didn't make sense to Leland. He was confused. "I don't get it," he said finally. "I told ya, no money, no gas."

"No, you don't get it. You don't turn that pump on for me, I'm gonna do something. Something you won't like," said the kid, head tilted up, looking over Leland's head at something.

"No shit. Like what?"

"Just do it, okay? I don't want to hurt you but I will. I promise I can and you won't like it."

"What? You got a gun or something? You know there's a camera up there, behind me? Getting all of this?"

"Turn around. Look at it," said the kid, with a toothy grin. But Leland just looked at the kid. He wasn't playing some game here, with this kid or with anyone. He sure didn't feel like turning his back on this nut. Leland looked closely at the guy. It dawned on him that he really was just a kid, despite being tall. "You better just get out of here. Best thing you can do right now. Just get!" Not for the first time, Leland wished there was a shotgun standing right there next to his leg, waiting to be picked up and pointed at assholes like this one. He'd even asked the boss-man if he could bring one in and put it there, just in case. Russell had just snorted and said no way.

The kid glanced up behind Leland before turning around and going out to his truck. He took out the nozzle and dropped it to the ground, then got in and gunned the engine and drove away fast.

Leland sighed a sigh of relief. Then he did turn around to reassure himself by looking at the camera. It must have been a trick of the light, or maybe what was left of his hangover, because instead of a camera, he saw something else hanging there from the mount. Maybe a small loaf of dark bread with a pickle sticking out the end. Or a large sausage. Or something. He just shook his head and turned back to face the door. "What the hell is wrong with me," he thought. The kid must have rattled him or something. He went out to the pump and replaced the hose. Then back inside to the coffeemaker to make a fresh brew. Back at the counter, he glanced at the place where the camera was supposed to be. This time, to his relief, it was the camera, just as it had always been. He chuckled to himself, shook his head and turned back around just as the door creaked and buzzed and a new customer came in. Bought some Marlboro's and a snack. The rest of the night was quiet.

MARTIN WAS MAD. That hadn't gone as he'd hoped but he couldn't blame anyone but himself. And that moron he'd threatened. And he still needed gas for the truck. There wasn't another gas station open around here for what, Twenty, thirty miles. He'd have to go up to the interstate probably. Unless he could get some money somewhere.

He was pretty happy with his camera trick though. It even made him smile. He hadn't even thought what to turn it into, just something else. He wasn't sure what it was it turned into, but it didn't matter. It wasn't a camera, so it wouldn't record what he told that guy.

But the guy wouldn't do what he wanted him to do. He really wanted to do something to him, just to see how it would go, but just as he was thinking what he might do, he remembered the rabbit. If he changed something in the guy, maybe gave him a funny nose or something, what would happen? Would it hurt him in ways Martin didn't expect? And if it was bad, it might kill him, and then he wouldn't get his gas, plus he'd worry about what that camera got before he changed it. It was smart, he thought, to hold back, not do too much until he knew what effects it was gonna have. There must be ways to make his powers pay for themselves. He just needed to figure out how. He needed to experiment. Practice. Get stronger. Then things would change for him. Then the world would really find out who Martin Conrad was.

Money. Martin wanted it. There must be a way to get it, with his powers. He couldn't think how though. Then he hit on an idea. He just needed a buck. One dollar bill. He searched the floor and the glove compartment of his dad's old truck and only found pennies. He was almost out of gas, but maybe he could get home. Then he could ask Sylvia for a dollar. Or Alice might have some money stashed somewhere. When he got home, it occurred to him to look in the garage for some gasoline. He found a small gas can about half full that Jack used to clean motor parts. He dumped it into his truck. That made him feel more sure that he could carry out his plan. He might have to drive up to the interstate to find a station, but now he could probably make it that far.

His plan was simple. Get a dollar bill. Go to one of the Quick Shops and pick out something cheap. Then, just before paying for it, imagine the dollar bill is really a much larger one, say a hundred dollar bill. Pay with that and pocket the change. He could do that as many times as he wanted. Shit, he could be rich in no time with that. Of course, he'd have to count on the counter guy putting the fake bill into his cash register first, then giving him change and not noticing later that the bill had changed back into a one-dollar bill. He wasn't sure how long it would hold its transformed shape, but it should be long enough.

But he still had to get that first dollar bill.

Sylvia wasn't home,. From the porch, he spotted her at the community garden. He went in her bedroom to find her purse.

No money there. He tried Alice's room. Finally he found some: three one-dollar bills hidden in a small drawer where she kept her socks.

Now equipped, Martin went back to his truck and drove back up the blacktop to 87. Instead of turning left to go to Jamestown, with its single gas station he had visited earlier, he turned right and drove up to I-70 to the big station on the left. He went in and picked out a cake covered with cinnamon sugar, and took it to the counter. He took out one of the bills and lay it flat, out of sight of the counterman, and stared at it hard. He tried to imagine it as a hundred- dollar bill. Then he realized he'd never seen one and had no idea whose picture was on it. He imagined just the numbers on it changing: the word "One" becoming "One Hundred" and the number going from 1 to 100. That worked, but it looked odd.

He tried to pay for the snack.

"What's this?" said the guy behind the counter. "A fake hundred? Not even a good one. Who you trying to fool, buddy?" The guy handed it back. "Nice try. That'll be a dollar-fifty- nine."

Martin snatched the altered bill and shoved it into his pocket. He pulled the other two out and paid and got the hell out of there fast. At least the guy didn't look like he was in the mood to call the cops or something.

He still had the one he had tried to change. Back at the truck, he pulled it from his pocket. It had already changed back to its original form. His mind was trying to work the problem. Maybe if he could get his hands on a real hundred, memorize what it looks like, he could get away with it. But what were the odds he could get one long enough for that, or at all?

Maybe just a picture of one would do? Where could he find that?

In a book maybe. He thought of the library in Booneville. He'd never been there – Jack wasn't much of a reader, only equipment manuals and such and he'd never taken Martin to a library. And his grandmother, who raised Martin when he was a kid, she'd never taken him anywhere except the casino. Still, it might be worth a try.

Finding it was harder than he expected. He drove around Booneville, up and down the main drag and some of the side streets until, frustrated and his gas gauge reading near empty, he pulled into the parking lot of the grocery store and went in to ask someone. He had trouble finding anyone who knew where the library was until he asked a gray haired lady working the checkout.

"Yeah hon, go on down the street, that way," she said, pointing to her left. "Look for a big church. It's right across the street. Can't miss it."

Martin tried to follow her directions but still didn't see any buildings that said "Library." He did pass a church, a big one, looked like some kind of Catholic cathedral or something. Glancing to the left as he passed, he saw a small one-story place with a sign that said "Booneslick Regional." It wasn't until he had turned around and was driving past the church again that he saw more of the sign around the side of the building: "Library."

The parking lot was empty. The building looked closed but he finally saw a sign on the door that said its hours were 9 a.m. to 6 p.m. Martin pulled open the door and went in. It took a while before he saw anyone. Finally, near the back, he spotted a young woman arranging books on a bottom shelf. She looked close to Martin's age, about 16 or 17.

"Hey," he said. "Can you help me find a book?"

Startled, she stood quickly, leaving an array of children's books by her feet. "Oh," she said. "I didn't know anyone was here. I'm just a volunteer. But maybe I can help." She faced Martin, looking nervous.

Martin liked what he was seeing. A lot. She had on skinny jeans. Looked poured into them. And a pink top that hardly held her boobs. Martin was spellbound, his mind racing, wondering if there was some way he could talk her into, you know, doing it with him. Having sex, right here. Or maybe convincing her somehow. But then he remembered what he was here for.

"A book about money. With pictures. Got that somewhere?"

The girl moved toward Martin to get out of the confines of the bookshelves, but Martin was slow to move. She stopped. "Excuse me," she said. "Let me out, I'll go look on the computer."

Martin stepped back, but only a little. He wanted her to have to squeeze by as close to him as possible. She did, moving as quickly past him as she dared. The smell of her dazzled Martin. He lifted his arm and just barely stroked her back as she moved past.

"Hey. What's your name? I'm Martin," he said, following her to the front of the library and the book checkout counter. "Are you by yourself here today?"

The girl remained silent. She put the counter between herself and Martin and sat down in front of the computer. She pressed a key and brought up a search screen. "About money? Let me see." She was silent as she searched, then, "Okay, go down to the aisle marked "References" and look for the Britannica reference book the the M's. She pointed to her left and looked at Martin, her eyes serious, her lips pursed. "That should have pictures, if that's what you're looking for." She held her arm up, pointing, her other hand on the telephone, until Martin finally moved off in that direction.

It did have pictures. They were old ones though. When Martin compared his one remaining dollar bill to the picture of one in the "US Currency" section of the encyclopedia, he was surprised to see there were many differences. The one in the book said it was a "silver certificate," whatever that might be. Then he looked at the pictures of the hundred dollar bill. It was very different from the one-dollar bill.

This looked harder than he expected. The bill was so detailed, and so different. How often would a clerk have seen one though? Maybe he wouldn't notice and just slide it under the money tray like he'd seen it done, because there wouldn't be a slot on top for a bill that large. Worth a try, he told himself.

He laid out his bill as before, stared hard at the picture and tried to imagine his bill looking like the one in the book. It worked, as he knew it would. But the result was disappointing: his bill sort of looked like a hundred, but it was now smaller and in shades of gray instead of multicolored black, gray, gray-green with tiny threads of other colors. The biggest problem, he thought, was the size. He picked it up and felt it between his fingers. It was thicker than a normal dollar bill too. It looked like Monopoly money. He imagined its background to be green, and to be larger; when it changed, it really looked like a Monopoly hundred, with an almost glowing pastel green background. The size looked better, though. Martin waited for it to change back. It took somewhere between a minute and two minutes, he guessed. It changed while he watched it, back to its original size and image. His attempt to resize it had made it noticeably larger than the original. He watched it pop back down to the correct size. This all made him tired. He figured he would need another dollar bill, sitting next to the one he wanted to change, so he could use it as a model to get a believable size and coloration. Martin shoved his bill back in his pocket and rose, leaving the book where it was. He headed back to the checkout counter, looking for the girl. She was not there. He then hunted all the aisles and areas for her. Nothing. She might be hiding in the bathroom. She might have left the building. Tired of hunting for a girl he knew wouldn't want to spend any time with him,

Martin walked out the library door.

WHEN MARTIN WENT BACK to his truck in the library parking lot, a white Ford Mustang pulled up next to him in the lot. Two young men got out and faced him. One, the driver, was hefty and tall. The other one was thinner and closer to Martin's size. They were dressed identically, black pressed slacks and button down white shirts. They wore identical necklaces holding the same simple thick crosses. Some sort of religious thing. His dad used to talk about them. Blamed them, along with blacks and Mexicans, for his not being able to get decent work at decent pay anymore. Black people and Mexicans, he said, had all the work because they were too stupid and slow to deserve good wages, so the farmers hired them instead of someone like Jack, who has all the experience and skills and deserved a decent living wage. Jack said they should all go back where they came from. And men like these, Amish and Mormons and Jews and such, were the worst. Jack had told Martin their secret societies held power over the government and they owned too much of the land around here. They hired their own kind and left people like his father out in the cold. "Hold it right there," said the driver. "Did you just come out of there? The library?" He nodded in the direction of his passenger on the other side of the car. "Hassling my buddy's sister?" The men walked toward Martin, one around the front of Martin's truck, the other around the rear.

"What? I wasn't hassling nobody," said Martin. Feeling

threatened, he remembered the length of pipe just under the seat of his truck, now out of reach.

The driver of the Mustang, pockmarked with short hair, stepped toward Martin from the front of his truck. He put a large hand on the side of Martin's truck door and gently pushed it shut, looking at Martin while he did it.

"No, see, we know you were in there messing with Joy. She called her brother there behind you and told us we needed to come have a talk with you. She's a sweet kid, Joy is. You don't want to mess with her. Her pop's a highway patrolman. You get on his bad side, you got real trouble."

Martin held the gaze of the big man. He felt anger rising. This is wrong, being put upon for no reason. Especially by people like these.

"I ain't done nothin'. You're the ones lookin' for trouble. You don't want to mess with me. You don't know what I can do."

The man looked down at Martin with a broad grin. By this time, the thin white guy had come up on Martin from the back. Without speaking, he came right up against Martin's back and put his arms all the way around him, pinning Martin's arms to his sides.

"What can you do?" said the big man. "Doesn't look to me like you can do much. Hold him still there, Todd. I'm doing a citizen's arrest of this guy for attempted rape."

Martin struggled. Todd, holding him, turned out to be stronger than he looked. Martin couldn't break free. "Don't! I'll hurt you!" he grunted. "This is just stupid. You don't know what I can do!"

The big man balled his fist and punched Martin in the gut, just above his belt. The wind went out of Martin and he had trouble taking another breath. As he doubled over, Todd let him go and Martin sank to his knees on the gravel. Still struggling to take a breath, he glanced up at the man. He thought, 'turn him into something else,' but he couldn't concentrate. And he didn't want to hurt the guy too much. Then he really would have the police chasing him.

"Get up," said the man, glowering down at Martin. "C'mon, on your feet, boy. We're not finished here."

Martin knew the safest thing might be to stay down, maybe even collapse onto his side like he was really hurt. But he was starting to breathe better. He struggled back up onto his feet.

"I think you need a lesson what happens to boys who go into the library and scare little girls." He formed a fist again and swung it at Martin. Martin had his eyes on the fist though, and in defense, quickly formed the thought, "soft". When the man struck Martin in the belly, he yelled in pain and drew his arm back. He held his hand up to his face. "What the hell!" he said, looking not at a hand, but at the flattened, floppy remains of a hand, boneless and shaking like jelly. Blood oozed out from around his fingernails. He stepped back in horror, his face contorted in fear and pain. "What the hell," he said again. "What did I hit?" He looked down at Martin's middle but it looked normal and unharmed. The man danced around, holding the remains of his hand in front of him, tears now streaming from his eyes. "Jesus, Todd. C'mon, drive me to the hospital. I don't know what the fuck he did, but it hurts like hell."

As the two men pulled out and roared away, Martin slowly got in his truck. He wasn't quite ready to grin at his victory, not yet. He had defended himself, but it was automatic, or something. He hadn't thought the thought, hadn't pictured anything except that hand coming toward him, accompanied by the realization that he didn't want to get hurt like that again. He must have willed the change, but he didn't remember doing it.

At last, hands on his steering wheel, he let his shoulders and abdomen relax. The danger was past. He had done what he said he was going to do – hurt the guy. And he was pretty sure it wasn't permanent. Or he hadn't killed the guy at least. For the rest, he didn't know how it would turn out. This was good. This was real progress, he felt. He had new respect for his powers now.

Feeling full of himself, he drove to the nearest filling station. It was another Quick Shop like the one in Jamestown. He was pretty sure he knew the layout. First, before going in, he peeked though the side window to see who was there. There weren't any other vehicles at the pumps or parking area, so maybe the clerk guy would be alone, as before. When he spotted the camera above and behind the cash register area, he imagined it to be something else: a plant of some kind. He watched as it transformed, turned green and drooped.

Martin walked in, didn't see anybody, not even the clerk, and walked around the counter and stood looking at the cash register. He didn't know how to get it open, so he started pushing buttons. To his surprise, the first one he pressed, an Enter key, popped the drawer open. Martin quickly scooped all the bills from the tray and pocketed them.

When the drawer opened, it rang a little bell. It wasn't much, but it was enough to bring the clerk, who had been out of site by the coffee maker. He looked at Martin and said, "Hey you, stop! You can't be back there!"

Martin, startled, said, "Don't come closer." The clerk did stop, briefly, then came toward Martin again. "Don't, I said." As the clerk reached the counter area, Martin, afraid of being caught now, blinked, and the clerk stopped where he was, unable to move.

Martin didn't know what he had done, but he knew he had

to get out of there fast. Within seconds, he was in his truck, gunning it out of the lot and toward the highway back down toward the river.

CHAPTER TEN

The Investigation Heats Up

KAREN CHAPMAN, DISPATCHER at the Moniteau County sheriff's office, was not having a good day. Her job was a great deal more than answering the phones and contacting Matt and his deputies when calls came for them. Who fixed coffee first thing in the morning? Who called the Culligan man when the big bottle in the break room was nearing empty? Who, in fact, acted as mother to a room full of professionals who sometimes acted like babies when things weren't going well?

The tone of the office stunk at the moment. Matt was dark and growly because there had been no progress on the Petersheim murder investigation in almost two weeks and the county prosecutor was calling almost every day asking for progress reports. Karen did her best to buffer Matt from that kind of pressure. But she knew how it was weighing on him. And now this: a letter to him from his wife's lawyer. Karen knew without opening it what it was: divorce papers. She hadn't given it to Matt yet but she couldn't wait forever. All he would have to do is sign them and return them. Karen was just waiting for the right moment.

What made it harder was the report Matt had just received from the sketch artist in Jefferson City. He had done his best to get a description from the victim's sister, but the result was next to useless. The girl was so distraught and confused, she couldn't give the artist anything without hiccuping and telling him it was wrong. So Matt was working blind. The truck they found near the scene was a dead end too. No one in Jamestown had been able to identify it. It was just too old and similar to dozens of others parked in farmer's yards or junked out to be useful.

THE PHONE RANG. Karen punched the button on her console to answer. It was a case worker at the Booneville hospital.

"Hi, is this the Moniteau County sheriff's office? I understand you all had a death involving bone injury, or something like that?"

"Yes m'am. Who would you like to speak to?"

"Well, whoever is looking into that? We had a man come in here complaining of something similar. I wondered if you all would like to take a look?"

Karen buzzed Matt, who was sitting in his office. "You might want to hear this," she said, then connected him to the case worker.

THE HOSPITAL WAS IN Cooper County, not his jurisdiction, but that didn't matter when it came to a murder investigation. Matt drove up to Booneville immediately. He spoke to the emergency room doc who had examined the man initially, then to the radiology doctor who showed Matt the film taken of the man's hand. He had called another specialist, an orthopedic surgeon, to join them in the x-ray viewing room.

"We've never seen an injury like this," said the radiologist.

"Have you, Jim?"

"I've seen film of bone crushed by a steam press, and some injuries from vehicle accidents, but nothing quite like this." He looked through the photos and notes from the intake team. "And look, there's no external injury resulting from trauma sufficient to crush bones. That's the strangest thing about this case."

"Could you send these images to our medical examiner? She has a body that may have similar damage. We've been at a dead-end with a murder case. This might help."

"Sure," said the radiologist. "I just need her email address."

"And I need to talk to the victim of this hand injury if possible."

FINDING THE VICTIM was easy enough. With no idea how to help the man with the strangely damaged fist, they chose to hospitalize him immediately to give their specialists a chance to examine him. Matt went up to the third floor. The man's room was at the end of the second corridor on the right. It was a large private room. Matt gathered his name and address from the charge nurse. One Daniel Everett Lloyd, the only son of the Lloyd family, well known for their large auto dealership. Matt had watched Daniel's father on television commercials for many years.

"Hello Daniel," Matt said. The victim, a young man in his twenties, was sitting up in bed. He said nothing and kept his eyes on the large flat-screen TV mounted high on the wall opposite. "My name is Matt Bettman. I'm sheriff of Moniteau County. How are you doing?" Daniel's right hand lay in his lap, encased in gauze wrapping that looked several inches think.

"Yeah, okay," said Daniel after what felt to Matt like a long pause to think about it. Probably on pain killers.

"Okay. That's good," said Matt. "I need to know ... can you

tell me what happened to your hand?”

“I told ‘em downstairs.”

“Tell me. Who did this? And how?”

“I don’t know what he did. I didn’t do nothin’ to him. Just talked. Then this happened.”

“Who? Do you know? Did you get his name?”

“No.” Daniel still kept his eyes on the TV. Matt glanced at it: nothing more than a commercial for toilet cleaner. “Was he alone? Where were you when it happened?”

“Library.”

“In Booneville?”

“Yeah, I guess.”

“You guess?” Matt’s patience was running out. “Look, I’m trying to help you here. I need you to talk to me. Help me find who did this to you.” Daniel exhaled with a whistle and looked down at his hand.

“I don’t know how you can help,” he said, finally looking over at Matt. “I can’t use this hand anymore. Doctor said he doesn’t know what happened to it and can’t see how I’ll ever be able to use it. And it’s my *right* hand!”

Matt couldn’t think what else to ask this man. Then, “What time did this happen? So you were in the library. Did whoever did this hit you or something?”

“Not in the library. In the parking lot. I hit him. Just once, in the stomach. Didn’t hurt him, really. He was being a butthole and he needed a lesson taught him. I was supposed to be that lesson. Then this happened. He didn’t touch me, not that I remember.”

“In the lot. Okay. How tall was he? How old? Did he have a car there?”

“Shorter than me, that’s all I know. Dark hair. Pretty young, like a teenager. And yeah, I remember his truck. Old pickup. Rusty. Dirty. My dad would kick my butt if I ever showed up in a junker like that.

 after interviewing Daniel Lloyd, Matt checked in with Karen at the station.

"Cooper County called. Said they knew you were chasing an odd case and they had one that might be down your alley. It's at the Quick Shop up there just south of the interstate if you want to check it out."

"What happened?" said Matt.

"Don't know. Robbery, they said, but the clerk said there was something unusual about it. You're close to there, aren't you?"

"Yeah, at the hospital. I'll drop by there. Anything else going on?"

"All quiet on the home front, Matt. Call me when you get there, okay? We all like to know where the boss is."

Matt looked at the hand-set before replacing it. He could see the grin on Karen's face. Not for the first time, he thought he should enforce a bit more discipline down in the office. But what the hell. Nothing wrong with a bit of family feeling, he supposed.

A was leaving when Matt pulled in beside the combo gas and food store at the intersection of 87 and I-70.

"How ya doin'," he said. "Word is you got a strange case, am I right?"

"I'm not sure what happened," said the deputy. A shuffling man nearing middle age, he looked to Matt like he needed a haircut. His badge said "Fischer".

"Mind if I go talk to the clerk?"

"Knock yourself out. I've got to get back to the station. I'm off in about five and my wife's expecting me to pick up groceries."

Matt found the clerk standing next to the register. "Hi, I'm sheriff down in the next county. They told me you had a problem here earlier today? Could I ask you about that?"

"Sure. Like I told that other policeman, I had a kid come in and hit the register while I was making coffee in the back. Took some cash and lit out."

"Hit the register? What does that mean?"

"He just opened it while I wasn't looking, is all."

"Okay. Don't you normally keep it locked when your not working the front?"

"C'mon. I do. I just didn't right then. I was only gonna be away for a minute. I told all that to the other guy and he made notes. Is this gonna get back to my boss? Insurance should cover the loss, right?"

"I don't have any idea. I just need to know what happened next. Did you try to stop the guy?"

"Yeah, I told him to stop. He just looked at me strange and then I froze."

"Froze? What does that mean?"

"Froze. Couldn't move. I mean, I wanted to, I was about to walk over the grab the kid by the collar and throw him out but when I got about, oh, three feet or so from him, it was like I was suddenly trying to walk through invisible jello or something. I couldn't move my legs or arms or speak or anything. Strangest damn feeling, I can tell ya. Lasted, oh, a couple minutes or so, then I could move normally again. By then, the kid had grabbed some money and headed out to his pickup."

"What kind of pickup, did you see?"

"Couldn't turn my head to see it. I mean I could just

glimpse it from the corner of my eyes. Dark. No paint. Rust. Pretty old. That's all I could tell."

Matt considered all this. Odd all right. It seemed likely it was the kid Lloyd ran into. "Let's take a look at your camera feed, okay?"

"Sure but it's no good. That other policeman played it back and it wasn't helpful. It was blank starting just before the kid came in and didn't come back on until just after he ran out and got in his truck."

"No kidding. Blank? As in nothing got recorded during the robbery, but it was okay before and after?"

"That's what we saw when he played it back."

"Wow. Okay. That's really strange." The clerk took him to the back office and played the file for him. Even though the visual went dark suddenly, then resumed after about three minutes, the time stamp continued on the bottom through the whole thing. Matt made notes of the time the blank part started and finished. He was about to leave when he took another glance at the computer monitor used to display the feed. He stopped when he noticed there were two sets of files listed. They all had dates and times in their file names, but there was one other difference, a dash followed by a number. Half the files had "-1" and half had "-2".

"How many cameras does this store have?" he asked the clerk.

"Just the one, I think." The clerk stopped to think. "Wait, no. There's one outside too. On the side of the front of the building. It watches the pumps."

"And probably sees who comes in and out," said Matt. He found the file for the outside camera with date and time name similar to the blank inside feed. When he played it, there it was, a little bleary and grainy, but it was what he was hoping to see:

an old farm truck next to a pump and a boy, dark hair and dark tee shirt, who looked about sixteen or so. Instead of going to the front door, the kid went to the window at the side for about thirty seconds, then went in the front. Two minutes later, he came back out, stuffing something in his jeans pocket and quickly pulled himself into the truck and sped off. The truck had no license plate. It was clearly the same truck he had inspected on the side of highway 87 the morning after the murder of the Petersheim man. He played the clip over and stopped it when he could see the boy's face. It wasn't a good image, but it was something. It was the murderer's face. He clicked the printer icon to print it out.

Matt arrived at the University of Missouri campus around noon. It had been many years since he had gone to school there. He was amazed at how large and complicated it had all gotten. Traffic was heavy. He had called Eve for directions to her lab but it still took a long time to find the building and then somewhere to park. He finally pulled down a slope to a garage door at the rear of a two-story glass and steel building near the center of campus and parked. He trusted the campus police to respect his vehicle with its Moniteau County Sheriff's logo on the side and lights on top, and not to tow it away. The door next to the garage door led to a hallway. Near the end he found himself in a glassed viewing area overlooking the main laboratory. Unlike Beth's autopsy room in the county building, this was a teaching facility. The autopsy lab was spacious. Below him and to one side, he spotted Eve in her white lab coat working on something on a movable table next to one of the several autopsy tables. She spotted him and waved him toward the side door leading to the lab.

"Welcome sheriff. Come on down please."

"I hope I'm not interrupting something important," Matt

said. "Not at all. I'm actually preparing some remains in order to show you something quite unusual." Matt went down four concrete steps onto the lab main floor and walked over to Eve.

"Where's the body? I thought you wanted to show me that." "It's in cooler storage. I have something better to share, and without the odors. Here, on this wall, check out the x-rays of the body. And then I'll show you this." She lifted a green cloth covering the remains of what might have been the Amish man's foot.

"First, the big one: the thorax and spinal area of the mid-body. You see this gray area? Looks out of focus? It's not. That's his ribs and sternum." She pointed with her finger to the area in the center of her chest. "That's over the heart, more or less. And that long smeared-looking mass is what's left of his spinal column. It looks out of focus because those bones, which should look like this...." She pointed to a second x-ray next to the first, "where you can see those same bones clearly. Notice the edges. They're still gray here, but intact. On your man, they're spread out. Like mush. They look like they're made of corn meal. That's the best description I can give you of their texture in this man. His bones were somehow disintegrated. Entirely."

She turned to the table where she had lifted the cloth. "This is his left foot. I've opened it to show what would normally be five solid bone in the center of the upper foot. You can see what's left of those bones. The largest piece is this one in the center - it's less then four millimeters in width. I've examined some of these bones closely. The ones this size appear to have been crushed into small aggregates, and then refused."

"Refused? What does that mean?"

Eve paused. "It's hard to explain, because it's impossible. Something we've never seen before. You know how, when you break a bone in your body, the doctor sets it — meaning she aligns the bones as they're meant to be and then immobilizes it — and lets it heal? Well, that healing normally takes several days for the body to knit the ends back together and form calcium deposits around the collagen. Eventually the bones rejoin. There can be bone-scarring and extra calcium. In other words, the bone heals by adding calcium, so there's usually extra bony material around the break.

"Now, the impossible part is this: it appears these bones were crushed, but they tried to knit back together. Though that description isn't right because there's no sign of the collagen knitting and calcium depositing. It's as if the particles of bone tried to rejoin to each other, to resume it's original shape, but failed to do so correctly. My theory is that, immediately upon disintegration, the spaces between the fragments was filled by fluids and the synovial material that normally surround the bones, preventing them from rejoining."

Eve pressed on the top of the mass with her gloved finger. Matt watched it press down and spring back. His breathing was ragged — the smells, he told himself. It didn't look like a foot.

The flesh was discolored and distorted. It reminded him of the fake hands he had bought for his son years back for Halloween.

"I think I understand what you're saying, but how is such a thing possible? And what will you put down as cause of death? I mean, best we can tell, he wasn't actually crushed."

"Right. There's no sign of the kind of skin and flesh damage we'd expect in a crushing event. This man's bones appear to be the only thing damaged. Cause of death would be either suffocation caused by the collapse of the chest cavity, or heart failure caused by pressure on the heart. Or both. Resulting from the loss of the ability of the rib cage to support the lungs and heart cavities. Though there's signs of major blood loss to the brain. But that might be a side effect of the heart losing its ability to pump effectively."

"My god. What happened to this man," said Matt, turning away. He was looking for somewhere to sit. He suddenly felt too heavy to stand.

"Please, over here," said Eve, leading him to a stool. The door above the lab opened. Cameron came down the stairs. "Hi Dad," said Eve, looking up. She kept her hand on Matt's shoulder. Then she looked in his eyes. "Are you feeling better?" Matt looked up sheepishly. "I'm fine. I missed breakfast this morning," he said, as if that explained his sudden dizziness. "I'm fine," he repeated, looking up at Cameron. "Good to see you, sir."

"Checking out the corpse, are we? A bit of a surprise, this one, eh?"

"To say the least," said Matt.

"Dad asked to come by to use my office. Apparently there are some internet issues where he lives."

"Right," said Cameron. "We called the provider's support people. They said they'd send someone out to check connections and sort the problem. Probably this afternoon. Meantime, I need to check my email and do a bit of research."

"We?" said Eve. "Who do you mean?"

"Well, there are others living down there at Able's Landing."

"But you had your own line installed."

"Mary Ellis is there. We're spending some time together. Talking."

"Talking? That all?"

"Darling. Prying. It doesn't become you," said Cameron. He turned to Matt. "How goes the hunt, sheriff?"

Matt stood and pulled a folded paper from his back pocket. "We got a break, I think. Kid pulled a robbery at a local gas station yesterday. It looks like he jimmied the inside camera somehow so we got nothing from that. But he must not have known about the camera mounted on the side of the building watching the pumps. Got this." He unfolded the paper and handed it to Cameron.

Cameron studied it for a moment. "So you think the truck in this picture may be a match for the one near the dead man's house?"

"It looks like it, yes, but there's more. This morning I talked to a young man who went to the emergency room with some kind of damage to his hand. The injury was similar to what Eve has been showing me here. He gave me a description. A kid, age, height and build match the description we got from the victim's sister. And this picture, fuzzy as it is. Oh, and the clerk on duty at the store reported something odd. He said when he tried to stop the kid robbing his register, he suddenly couldn't move. Just froze when the kid looked at him. It only lasted a short while. He estimated five minutes or so then he was okay. But by then the kid had gone."

Cameron whistled. "Very interesting. You have been busy, Matt. That's a good day's work, I'd say. What's next?"

"I thought I'd drop down to Jamestown and ask around. See if anybody recognizes this truck and the perp."

"Of course. I'd like to join you if you don't mind. But I've got to do some work here first."

"I'll call you if I get a lead on who this kid is. We can go try to find him together."

"Right. Good plan. It's not a good idea to approach this person without some backup, even if he is a kid." Cameron turned to his daughter. "Care to speculate on the mechanism involved in all this? Since we've never seen this before, wild-ass guesses are appropriate."

Eve pointed to the mutilated foot on her tray. "My analysis suggests something new is happening. Something we've never seen before. I was explaining to Matt that the injury resembles bone crushing, but then something happens to the bones: they appear to try to fuse immediately. Dad, that's not possible. The science is just not right. It's like microscopic clumps of bone are forced to separate, then if they are close enough together, they try to reform into their original shape. There are bones in this man's head that appear to have rejoined successfully. But in all the samples I've examined, the result is wrong. Catastrophically bad in fact. The bones granulate and almost become fluid. All other tissue is normal but the body looses its entire support structure and collapses, causing all internal organs to fail, including lungs and heart." Eve stood still, facing her father. "I'm afraid my knowledge and imagination fail beyond that, dad. I can't imagine what sort of force could do a thing like this."

As Cameron positioned himself before Eve's bank of computer screens, there was one thought in his head: solving every mystery begins with figuring out the right questions to ask. It was Detective 101, actually, but he was amazed how often he had had to remind his supervisors and their detectives of this principle. And himself. Teach your people, he would say. Remind them of the fundamentals, which so often got swamped in details and politics. To solve major crimes, allow yourself to be curious. Solving a crime is solving a puzzle. Find all the missing pieces and fit them together, he would tell his people, to their annoyance. Stuck on a case? Go back to the beginning. Lay out the facts, separate what you think you know from what you actually know. Follow the facts. Determine which questions you've overlooked. Get off your ass and go find the answers. He opened a small text document to use as a scratch pad. He began typing in key phrases.

Next, he opened tabs in Eve's browser for each search phrase. He copied each phrase into the address bar and pressed Enter. He quickly scanned the top results for each page, looking for two things: links to the same pages, and hints to the next set of questions to ask.

There was some crossover for the phrases "Unexplained injuries" and "Unexplained deaths." He right-clicked on those links and opened them in new tabs. The last three phrases led to an endless rabbit-hole of sites dealing with dark powers, Goth games and sites, and tracts apparently written by Ph.D candidates in various religions. For "Bone disintegration" he found primarily sites related to dentistry. The results for "Unusual abilities" and "Temporary paralysis" were more interesting. He crosschecked those with the pages he had saved from "Unexplained injuries" and "Unexplained deaths".

After about an hour, Cameron emerged from his hunt, his head spinning. The pages he drilled down to revealed a wealth of events, unconnected but world-wide that suggested strange powers emerging. Strangest of all, those powers seemed to be manifesting in children and teens, up to puberty or a bit later. News reports, especially from less-developed countries where journalism seemed freer to report on unexplained events, showed unrelated reports of deaths, both of kids and adults, due to strange changes in their bodies. Adults, including police and militia, who try to control them sometimes experienced unexplained resistance, including paralysis and death and, oddly, disappearances. Children in cities, especially densely populated centers like Calcutta, had formed roaming gangs that mostly kept out of site of authorities. They seemed to be led by older teenagers. Cameron found a report written by a Chinese journalist in Taiwan who appears to have gained the trust of a group of children there. His report was respectful of their powers and of their intentions. His profile of their leader, a young man of sixteen, described them this way: "Guan Wei told me his job was less that of a leader than that of a teacher. The abilities of the children under his watch was a danger to themselves and others. He hoped to guide them toward understanding and controlling their abilities to manifest matter and energy before they were damaged by these abilities. If he succeeds, he expects the group will be able to establish a community and school for others with these emerging powers."

Manifesting matter and energy. However unexpected or even miraculous these emerging abilities might be, this seemed to match what was happening in Moniteau county. A boy, sixteen, with powers he doesn't understand, reacting to circumstances over which he has little control, would be dangerous indeed.

Something was going on all right. Something worldwide and huge and strange and dangerous. Something that could destroy everything. Or maybe the opposite: something with the potential to solve most of the ills of the world.

Cameron stepped out of Eve's office. He had to share what he had learned with her. But first, he opened his cell phone and called Sheriff Matt Bettman.

WHILE DRIVING SOUTH, Matt inventoried in his mind what he had to go on so far. A vague description from the dead man's sister. An old pickup truck located near the scene. The physical damage to the victim and to the man with the damaged hand. Then the sighting of the pickup truck and the dark-haired boy getting in it. That was about it. Dammit, Matt chided himself. He'd been sloppy. He should have posted a deputy to watch the truck, try to see who picked it up. Hindsight. It was way late to be thinking about that. At least he had a printout of the truck and boy, from the rear but better than nothing. At least he could show that around to folk in Prairie Home and Jamestown, the two largest towns between Booneville and California on route 87, which seemed to be where the boy and truck had been seen the most.

He visited the Evergreen Tavern and Carolyn's Cafe in Prairie Home first. It was too early in the day for many to show up at the tavern, but the cafe was just getting busy with lunch service. He walked past each table, showing the picture and asking folk if they recognized the vehicle or the boy. He knew some of the folk there too, so he chatted up some old friends.

"Anyone?" he asked the four older folk at one table, farmers in faded overalls and boots with the worst of the mud knocked off, grizzled cheeks rubbed clean for their lunch gathering after a long morning of work, with rough hands and dirt under their nails.

"Well maybe," drawled one, squinting at the black-and-white picture Matt held. Then, "No sir, I guess I don't know who that is. Truck looks familiar though. I used to have one lot like that."

"Yeah?" said Matt. "What happened to it?"

"Well, two or three years ago I traded it off to Jack Conrad for some dirt work he did for me. Dug out an overgrown pond. I remember he had an ancient dozer. I swear I've never seen one so old 'cept at the state fair. Broke down a lot. He spent most of his time tryin' to keep the damn thing running instead of pushing dirt with it."

"Okay. Jack Conrad. Any idea where he lives?" said Matt.

"Seems to me he moved on or something. Haven't seen him in ages. Used to have a family though, down Wolf's Point way I believe he said."

"Thanks Bill."

MATT DROVE DOWN through Jamestown and decided to take Fox Hollow over to Wolf's Point. If he didn't find anything, he'd go back over to the Evergreen later in the day, after the day workers got finished and before they headed home for supper, then the little pool hall in Jamestown on the way back to California.

He radio'd Karen in the office. "I got a possible lead on that truck. I'm going on over to Wolf's Point to see if I can find Jack Conrad's family. I should be back before y'all go for the day, hon."

Fox Hollow Road was paved about halfway down to the river, then it turned to gravel. It curved left to follow the ridge line of the hills above the Missouri all the way over to route P, which went down to the little town at the bottom of the valley between two creeks. Matt had been to Wolf's Point a few times over the years, mostly to enjoy the river there during the annual chili festival the town held each year to pay the town light bill. That party had gotten pretty big over time. He decided it was his job to make sure there was no trouble when the mass of people showed up from Columbia and surrounding areas. The chili and pie made by the locals was pretty good too.

Around halfway to Wolf's Point, Matt passed a gravel road to his right with a sign, Garrett Road. He glanced at an abandoned two story house a few hundred yards down. He'd seen it many times over the years while driving the back roads, his favorite way to relax while actually doing something useful in what was otherwise a mostly uneventful job. The house was abandoned but not crumbling, not yet. With a good bit of restoration it could be made livable again. It would hardly be worth the cost though, unless it were done by someone handy with a hammer and saw.

Every time Matt saw a place like that, and there seemed to be a lot of them in this part of the county where the land was rocky and steep and not suited to farming or even raising livestock, he wondered if he might be the guy to fix up a place like this. It would be cheap enough to buy and just hold for his retirement, if he didn't wait too long. Price of land all over the county was going up. Too many people, even in dirt-poor Moniteau County. They all wanted a piece of the American pie, just like Matt did. And why not. People work hard, mostly, for what they get in this part of the country. They deserved some comfort and peace and quiet in their waning years. It was why Matt was doing what he was doing, after all. Keeping the peace. He was a peacekeeper. Remembering why he had taken up law enforcement once in a while made him feel warm and satisfied that he'd made a good career choice, even though he seemed to have gone about as far has he was likely to go in the profession. It was okay though. He was okay.

As he passed the house, he glanced again at the place to see how the back of it was holding up. Something caught his eye. An old pickup truck, parked out of sight of the road. *The* old pickup truck, by the look of it. He slowed to a stop and put his 150 in reverse and backed slowly until he could turn down Garrett Road.

Matt turned into the drive to the abandoned house and stopped well short of the front door. The place looked dead, all the windows blank and showing nothing but darkness inside. The front door was in the center of the house with only a stoop and a single stair, a traditional style common in the mid-nineteenth century, with chimneys on both ends and no porch. A house that old, built of clapboard with hand-cut shingles, would be long gone in early twenty-first century. This one had likely been built more recently, maybe 50-60 years ago, Matt estimated.

He reminded himself why he had stopped here. If the boy he was hunting was here, he, Matt, could be at risk. He should call for backup before even getting out of his truck. But it was a long drive up from California, or even down from Booneville, which was in a different county anyway, and what if he was wrong about the truck?

Matt got out and shut the door as quietly as possible. It was silly to try to be quiet, he told himself, but nonetheless. If the boy was here, if he were armed, or whatever he had used to hurt the man with the broken fist, surprise might be Matt's best chance to take him. He reached down his right hand and loosened the strap over the grip of his service weapon.

He walked quietly around the side of the house, staying low when he passed the two windows, until he reached the corner. He stuck his head out to see the truck, like the cops do on the TV shows. Out and back, real fast like a snake. He glimpsed the back of the truck but didn't see the boy. He unholstered his gun and stepped out, raising his gun with both hands. He felt a little silly in this posture; it was a TV cop thing again, a city cop thing. But Matt had never been in a situation like this, had almost never had cause to unholster his weapon, almost never genuinely felt threatened. This was different. A new one, facing something as unknown as this boy with whatever ability he might have to hurt someone.

He stepped forward, watching the back of the house, watching the truck. No sign of the boy until ... he saw him step out the back door of the house holding something in his hands. A young man, maybe sixteen, short, dark hair — the description matched.

"Stop! Don't move!" Matt yelled. He held the gun up.

The boy, startled, dropped whatever he was holding and turned toward Matt. He looked up at him with a terrified look. Then his face scrunched up as if he were in pain, and said, "Don't! Please!"

For Matt, the moment was a surprise. Unexpected. Something was wrong. He could no longer hold his hands up in front of himself. He could no longer hold his body up. He could see the earth moving up toward his face but he couldn't turn away, couldn't avoid the blow to his nose and eyes. He crumpled forward, and down, like a suddenly deflated balloon or an accordion made to collapse. Down he dropped. He expected to feel his knees touch the ground first but even that didn't happen. He was wide awake and more alert than he could remember ever being. There was no pain, then there was a hint of a burning feeling. It was all so wrong. So impossible. He suddenly remember turning a corner and coming upon a fellow soldier in Afghanistan who was sprawled like this. He didn't want it. He tried to hold himself up but his arms seemed to have no strength.

The next moment, all he could see was the dirt next to his eyes and felt fear as he realized he was no longer able to breathe.

CHAPTER ELEVEN

Cameron Takes Over

EVE STEPPED INTO HER OFFICE. She hung her white lab coat to a hook on the wall next to the door. "I'm going to lunch, dad. You want to go?"

Cameron looked up from Eve's computer. "I'd like that, darling. But I promised Sheriff Bettman I'd drive down and join him in the hunt for that young man and his truck. I'm not comfortable with him going alone. Next time I'm in town, okay?"

"Of course. Go. I'll close up behind you."

Outside, he turned his phone on and found Matt's number. He smiled and waved as Eve got in her new car, the shiny orange and white Mini Cooper S.

Matt's number went directly to voice mail. "The person whose phone this is is unavailable...." Odd, Cameron thought. The phone must be turned off.

He looked up the number for the Moniteau County sheriff's office. He touched the number and his phone auto-dialed it. To get past the predictable recording, "If this is an emergency, hang up your phone and dial 911 ...." Cameron touched zero. After a moment a woman's voice responded. "Moniteau County Sheriff. How can I direct your call?"

"This is Cameron Sheffield. Is Sheriff Bettman there please?" "He's not here at the moment. Can I direct you to a deputy?"

"Thank you, no. I'm assisting him on a case. I was with him about an hour ago. He said he was going to try to find a vehicle spotted in a surveillance tape. I think he said he was going to Jamestown. Does that sound right? Do you happen to know where I can find him?"

"You're the English detective? He told us he was working with you. He called in not long ago. Said he was going to go over to a town next to the river to look for it. Wolf's Point. He's looking for someone named Jack Conrad. There's only twenty-some-odd people live there. It should be easy enough to locate him."

"Thanks for the help. I'll find him. Is anybody with him? A deputy?"

"No, it's just him. He likes it that way. Besides, we don't have a lot of deputies. Just the two, and he likes them to be here when he's out, in case someone calls for help."

"I understand. But it's always good to have backup when you're out looking for a bad guy."

"Well, yes, I suppose it is. It's just that we haven't had a lot of bad guys lately that needed hunting up."

Cameron sat in his BMW, turned on the engine and said "Hey Google." The screen of his dash radio formed a squiggly question mark. He said, "Map Wolf's Point Missouri." The display changed to a large map with a red dot showing his destination. It was right next to the broad blue line indicating the Missouri River, about two miles north of his home at Able's Landing, on the other side of the river. He touched the Navigation option and his radio began issuing instructions leading him up to I-70 west.

After about an hour of driving through rural hills surrounded by fields and forests, a series of steep drops took him from the high plains to the river bottom land. Wolf's Point appeared after a sharp curve to the right. Suddenly Cameron was in the tiny town. The dispatcher was right: it was not much more than five graveled streets and a few houses. He continued toward the river and stopped in front of a small cinder block building with a sign that said "City Hall". The single room was empty but around back, he found a blond haired woman planting flowers along the side of a small deck with benches.

"Hello," he said. "I'm looking for the county sheriff. I was told he might be down here somewhere."

The woman clapped the dirt from her gloves and rose to her feet. "Hi," she said. "I haven't seen any police down here. Not in a long time, actually." She pulled off her gloves and extended her hand. "I'm Sylvia."

Cameron took her hand and squeezed it gently. "Cameron Sheffield. I'm a detective with ... no one really. Retired. But I've been asked by the state's attorney general to assist with an investigation. I'm helping Matt Bettman. I was told he was coming here to speak with Jack Conrad. Do you know where he lives?"

The woman smiled and looked down. She put her gloves on the rail of the deck. "Do you mind if we sit? All this squatting has my back in an uproar. I need to rest it for a while." They stepped up on to the deck and sat on the bench that ran around the perimeter. "Now," she said. "It's funny you should ask about Jack. He was my boyfriend until, oh, almost a year ago now.”

“Really.”

“Yes, and I sort of threw him out. I have a daughter, she’s nine, and he was, let’s say, not a nice man. So he moved out. I don’t know where he lives now. He left his son here though. He’s about sixteen and not the brightest bulb in the pack. We live in that house on stilts at the corner before you turn down this street,” she said, pointing past Cameron’s car.

“I see. So maybe you can tell me, does he have an old gray pickup truck? What they call a farm truck, with no license?”

“Jack you mean? I believe so. Did have anyway. I think Martin has it now, though he’s not licensed. But that’s never stopped him from driving it.”

“Thank you Sylvia. You’ve been more than helpful.” Cameron started to rise when the door to the back of the town hall opened and a young woman came out. She carried a pair of gardening gloves and a hand rake.

“Sorry I’m late,” she said, waving the hand with gloves to Sylvia. “It took Alex a little while to settle down after her breakfast. Adele said to go ahead and come help you.”

“Hey Anna. This is detective, uh, what was your name?”

“Sheffield. Cameron Sheffield.” He stood as Anna stepped up to the deck and sat down next to Sylvia. “Gardening too? I expect I’ll be taking that up soon, too. I just moved into a houseboat over at Able’s Landing.”

“Interesting,” said Anna. “Gardening on a houseboat. How does that work?”

“Small flower boxes under the windows, I suppose. The former owner suggested it. And there’s room on the ground above the dock. I’m responsible for that too, so I’ll want to free it of weeds and make it inviting.”

“Detective Sheffield came down looking for the county

sheriff. Something about the old truck Martin's been using. So, has he done something?"

"Possibly," said Cameron. He pulled out a card holder and gave Sylvia a card. "Could you call me when Martin returns?"

"Sure. He disappears for days at a time though." Anna said, "So you're looking for Martin? Has he done something wrong?"

"Why, do you think he might have?"

"I don't know him well," Anna said. "But of all the people I've met down here, he seems the most likely to get into trouble."

"Why do you think that?"

"Oh, I don't know." She looked over at Sylvia. "Just a feeling I guess. Something about the way he looks at me. And my daughter. He made me really nervous. But I can't really say I know him."

Sylvia said, "Anna's right. The boy's wasn't raised very well. And his dad's no example to live by, I can tell you that. When he left, he didn't bother to take Martin with him. He just expected me to take care of him. I do the best I can, but he's a loner and won't listen to me about anything. I don't know what happened to his mother, but his father is just an ... excuse me ... a major league asshole. He's never liked the boy, and made almost no effort to care for him when he was here. Stupidest thing I've ever done, taking up with Jack. And Martin's grandmother — he apparently lived with her for years before coming down here with his dad — she was even worse, from what I've heard. A drunk and a gambling addict. She tried to control him I guess but she never even had enough to feed him, and Jack was always off doing something or other. Anyway, I shouldn't speak evil about her or him. It's not Martin's fault, but he doesn't have enough horse sense to take care of himself, so it's likely he has done something. Not for the first time either. He has been in juvie more than once for truancy and stealing."

"You know," said Anna, "I was talking to your daughter yesterday. This may not be related but she told me something that bothered me." Anna looked troubled. "It might be nothing. But Alice said she was watching Martin from her bedroom. He was out on your deck, holding a baby rabbit by the legs over the rail. Like he was thinking about dropping it. The rabbit was wiggling like crazy, she said, then it jerked suddenly and stopped moving. She said Martin must have hurt it or something because she saw blood coming from its mouth. But he hadn't touched it with his other hand. He had that behind his back. Alice said the rabbit jerked or jumped or something, she couldn't see it clearly, and then it looked different. She said Martin dropped it then and when he turned around, he was smiling. A crazy kind of smile, was how she put it. She said she felt afraid of Martin then. Anyway, Martin left in his truck and when Alice went down to look at the rabbit, it was like it had been gutted and half-skinned. Almost like it was turned inside out. It was horrible. She didn't want to leave it there, so she dug it a shallow grave and put it in it."

Anna looked down then back up at Sylvia. "Thanks for telling me," said Sylvia, though she looked pale. "Yes, thanks, Anna," said Cameron. "Odd as it sounds, I've read recently about similar stories. Something seems to be happening to certain young folk. Some, it seems, have developed the ability to do things with their minds. I wonder if that may explain what Martin did to the rabbit?" With that, he rose and excused himself. "I've got to go find Sheriff Bettman."

Jess had spotted Cameron's BMW parked next to the town hall. Then he saw him coming around from the back. He knew he had to talk to him. "Hey! Hi," he said breathless, coming up to Cameron. "I know why you're here. You're going to need my help!" Cameron stopped and looked at this serious young man. He was just a boy, sure, but there was something about him. Cameron's gut seemed to say, stop, wait, listen to what he has to say.

"Okay. What is it? Why am I here and how can you help?"

"Martin," said Jess. "He lives here. You're looking for him. And for someone else too."

"How can you ...."

"I just know. I can ... anyway, they're both at the same place. I can take you there if you take me with you."

"I don't know, son. Who are you anyway? I could be in lot of trouble if I let you go with me."

"My name is Jess. I live up the street. I know things. I can do things." Cameron stopped. He remembered what he had read about children worldwide showing new abilities. Perhaps this boy ....

"Okay, but still ..."

"Close your eyes. Let me show you." Cameron sighed. Then he closed his eyes. Instead of darkness, it was as if he were in a different place, in darkening twilight. He felt, more than saw, the mass of a building next to him on his right. Below him, a darker mass, twisted, not moving. He seemed to move closer to the mass. Two things struck him: the mass was a body, shaped like the body of the Amish man on Eve's table. The other thing was the gleam of a silver badge. It was vague, he couldn't read it, but the shape was a familiar one. It looked like the badge Matt wore on the pocket of his shirt.

With a sudden intake of breath, Cameron opened his eyes and looked at Jess. "All right," he said. "What was that?"

"I'll show you. Let's go." Jess didn't hesitate. He opened

the passenger door of the BMW and got in. Cameron, slower, finally got in.

"I told you, I can't take you with me. Just tell me which way to go."

"There isn't time. He's still there."

"Who?"

"Martin. He'll leave if we don't hurry."

Gritting his teeth, Cameron started the car and pulled out to the blacktop out of town. He had to take the chance. He would take the boy back as soon as possible and apologize to the boy's parents if needed. Just up the road before the big hill rising to the upper plains, Jess urgently pointed to a gravel road to the left. "There!"

Cameron turned onto it, the Beamer fishtailing on the loose gravel. He picked up speed, slowing down only for the sharp turns bordering farm property.

"Where?" he said. "How far?"

"I'll show you," said the boy. "Faster!"

"I can't go faster on these roads, lad. These curves are dangerous enough as it is." Each time they passed a driveway or side road, Jess stared at it intently. Finally, they drove past a road with a sign: Garrett Road. Jess was looking hard at a house just down the road.

"There! Go back!"

Cameron braked to a skidding stop and reversed until he could turn onto the side road. As he did, he could see the house and the black F-150 with the Moniteau County Sheriff logo on the driver's door parked in front of it.

"Damn," he breathed. "That's Matt's truck. I never would have seen that. Well done, son." He slowed and turned into the drive. He pulled up next to the black truck.

When he started to get out, Jess reached out his hand and

held onto Cameron's arm. "Wait," he said."

"Why?"

"Too dangerous. He's right there, in the house, looking at us. He could hurt you too." Cameron sat quietly. He realized he'd made the same mistake Matt had made. Martin might be a boy of sixteen, but the evidence suggested he had powers. Lethal powers. If the vision he had had of Matt on the ground, a twisted, collapsed mass, was true .... He could only hope it was no more than a warning.

In his former life as a chief detective, he would have had the resources he needed. He could call in for backup. Additional constables or an armed emergency response team. Here, he had nothing but his cell phone. He could call the highway patrol department at the state capital, but it would take forever for anyone to get up here. And he would be hard pressed to provide his location. He heard Jess say, "Wait here. Don't get out. Don't worry about me." When he looked to his right all he saw was the passenger door open and close, apparently on its own volition.

Martin stared through a smudged window with a ragged curtain at the driveway in front of the house. He watched the car pull into the drive and park next to the sheriff's black truck. It was like watching a movie, a slow, sad movie, with no plot. He felt stiff and sick to his stomach. He didn't want to move, didn't want to stand, didn't want to sit. Lying down, that might feel good, but he needed to see who was in the car and what they would do. He had been having waves of nausea and dizziness since coming in the house after being threatened by the sheriff. It was over quickly, the confrontation. Like it had been the night he tried to get help, get gas for his truck. He not only didn't get help, he got attacked. He didn't know what he did to protect himself, but it had stopped the attack. Just like here, only minutes ago. Or was it hours? He couldn't tell. Time seemed flexible. Or his ability to know how long things took was flexible. Something about his mind had started changing. When Alice showed him those mushrooms and challenged him to make things happen with his mind, and he tried and found he could do it, make things into different shapes, at least for a while. Then it was like he had entered a dark house, like this one but darker and stranger with all kinds of corridors and doors and windows that looked out to nothing but gray wasteland. And he was still there, in that place, trying to find a way back to the world he had known.

Martin reached out and grasped the loose handle to the front door. He twisted and pulled. It resisted but finally opened. He stepped out onto the porch. Loose boards, he could feel them but could barely see them when he looked down. There was a roar in his head too, a rumbling sound like some kind of machinery, like the sound Jack's old bulldozer made when he started it up and before he pushed it into gear. Like the sound of a whole hive of bees hovering next to his ears. He couldn't tell if it was real.

He stood looking out at the grass and gravel with the truck and the shiny new car with the big man sitting in it, looking at him. He was only mildly curious who he was and why he didn't get out.

He sat down on the porch and dangled his legs into the weeds below. There were other sounds too: a dry wind, and creaking boards and snapping twigs and something that sounded far away, like a fire maybe. Then he heard a voice next to him. Like someone was speaking right into his ears, both of them, or maybe right into his mind. He couldn't tell. He didn't much care which it was.

"Martin," the voice said. "It's Jess. I want to help you."

Martin looked around, both sides and behind him. He saw no one. "It's okay. You're safe. No one wants to hurt you." The voice was quiet, soothing. Martin wanted it to be true. He was so tired. Right now, he just wanted to lean over and put his head in Jess's lap and take a nap.

"People keep trying to hurt me," he whispered.

"That's over now," said the voice. "I'm going to take you to a safe place. No one will threaten you there. You'll be with people like you. They'll help you learn how to use your abilities to do good things."

"I just want to sleep now," said Martin. "I think I'll just go lie down on the seat of my truck. It's out back. I can sleep there, I've done it before." Martin started to get up, but he felt weak. So weak, so sleepy. He couldn't do it. He put his hand down on the porch beside him and leaned on it, trying to lever himself to his feet. "I can't ...."

Suddenly he felt very light. It felt almost like flying. He tried to open his eyes, but he was so very sleepy ....

CAMERON HAD BEEN WATCHING MARTIN. He saw him talking to someone. To himself, he presumed, as he was alone. Where had Jess disappeared to, he wondered. Then, as he watched, he saw something he never expected to see: Martin had tried to get up, then he seemed to disappear. Had he blinked? Maybe Martin had moved away so fast Cameron couldn't follow with his eyes. It was the sort of trick he knew master magicians employed to fool the eye. But he could see the entire porch and the yard in front of it. Had his attention wavered? The boy he had been hunting was nowhere to be seen.

Moments later he saw Jess, walking back to the car. He walked slowly, from the porch. Cameron opened his door and stood beside it, watching Jess.

"Where did you go? And where did Martin go? I was

watching him and then I couldn't see him."

"He's gone." said Jess. He looked sad. "He won't hurt anyone again, I'm sure. He didn't mean to hurt anyone, I'm certain. He just reacted when he thought someone was going to hurt him, and he made things happen without knowing what he was doing."

Cameron walked around the side of the house. As he turned the corner to the back yard, he saw it. The mass on the ground that Jess had shown him. He squatted and looked closely. It was Sheriff Matt Bettman all right. At least he looked peaceful. There was no sign of fear or pain on his puffy, lined face. But he was distorted and collapsed, just like the Amish man. And he was stone cold to the touch.

CHAPTER TWELVE

New World

MARTIN HAD BLINKED, that's all. Jess was talking to him but he couldn't see him and he thought, "he's invisible," which after all that happened to him didn't seem so impossible. Then he closed his eyes, just to see if he might see Jess when he opened them again. He didn't, but he saw something even more unexpected.

He was no longer sitting on the rotting porch of the rotting house in the putrid river bottoms. The first thing that struck him was the smells. He was so used to the smells of rotting vegetation along the bank of the Missouri that he no longer noticed it. But now he was noticing a new smell: something delicious. Something wonderful. The uplifting fragrance of flowers and freshly mown grass and something new. The salty odor of what he knew must be the sea. Salty and refreshing and with its own kind of rot, but not unpleasant like the smells near his home.

He looked around. He was standing in a wide meadow. No,

a lawn, long and wide bordered by flowers on all sides but one. The side toward the ocean — he heard surf now — was bordered by trees that reached to the sky and blossomed wide with palm leaves. Their trunks, lean and golden brown and slightly arched, swayed gently with the wind. This, he realized with a start, was not Missouri. No longer hills and limestone and swampy creeks and sinkholes. This was something — somewhere — else. How had he got here?

He stood still, not ready to move until he'd taken it all in. He closed his eyes again and opened them, this time hoping he would not go somewhere new. He liked this place, however he had got here. It was new, but new in a good way.

Then he noticed people walking toward him. It seemed a lot of people, wearing shorts and colorful shirts. As they neared, he saw they were young. Boys and girls, different ages and sizes, all walking toward him. In the lead was a tall young man. Martin could tell from his face the man was close to his age. His skin was dark but his features were narrow, like Martin's own. Unlike most of the rest of the group, he wore tan trousers and a white short sleeve shirt with some kind of embroidery on the front in the same color as the shirt. He carried a single flower in his left hand, dark blue or purple with a long stem, and led the others. He looked directly at Martin as he came near. He stopped about ten or fifteen feet from Martin and all the children with him began to spread out to both sides, forming a half-circle around Martin. No one spoke.

Finally, the leader said, "Please, let's all sit." He folded his legs beneath him and lowered his body to the lawn without using his hands. Then all the children, for they were all younger than he, similarly lowered themselves. Most had to reach down with arms and hands to steady themselves, but some sat gracefully, as the leader had done.

The leader held his eyes on Martin. "Welcome to our home," he said. "I am Guan Wei. You are safe here. We are your friends, Martin. You will be living with us now." He paused and spread his arms out in both directions. "I'm sure you must have questions."

Martin opened his mouth but couldn't figure out what to say. Finally he squeaked, "Where am I? How did I get here?"

"Where isn't important. You are in a safe place, as I said. This is a kind of school, for people like you. How you got here — well that's not an easy question to answer. You'll understand in good time. You have a great deal to learn, in fact. What I can tell you is that you are a part of the new generation of humans who will change history. You are important, Martin. Everyone here has unique abilities, like you."

Martin's breathing had sped up and he found tears had sprung to his eyes. He only now began to realize how frightened he had been of life, how threatened everything seemed to him, how unloved. That it might be possible that all that could change for him ... it was overwhelming. "Take your time," said Guan Wei. "Soon we'll go back to the house and have some food. I'll introduce you to the others and we'll find you a place to sleep." He stretched his arms in front of him, toward Martin, palms up, and rose to his feet effortlessly.

"Welcome home, Martin Conrad."

While the other children gathered around Martin and walked toward the home at the end of the lawn, Guan Wei stayed behind, watching them. When they were some distance away, he said, "Are you ready to join us too?"

Jess appeared, sitting comfortably on the lawn looking toward the ocean.

Guan Wei sat beside him. "You're the one, aren't you. I've been wondering when we might meet," he said.

"This is a good thing you're doing, Guan Wei. Helping these children adjust to their new life. And you're doing more than that. I can feel it, this expanding network you're building. The connections, even if the children aren't yet aware of it. Linking their minds to the rest of the emerging humans. Raising the intelligence of all of them, even the ones who have no idea what you're doing."

"It's an effect," said Guan Wei. "Not intentional, but a good thing, I think. The inevitable result of the opening of mankind's consciousness. It's part of our education, all of us. Even you, I imagine, are part of this emerging consciousness."

"Even me, yes. It's how I knew about your school, about what you're doing. It's what led me here. With Martin. These linked lines of consciousness are raising the intelligence level of all people everywhere now. Even the older ones. We will begin to solve the damage done to the species in the beginning. The age of the sword is coming to an end. But there are dangerous times ahead for those left behind. Part of what we must do, part of what you must teach the children, is how to protect the legacy beings, our ancestors. They won't understand, most of them, and they will react.

"About Martin. You must know he's damaged, that he'll need a great deal of care to emerge properly. And that if you can give him that, he will be a powerful force for good in the world eventually."

"I suspected, yes." Guan Wei rose and stood looking toward the house. "Won't you join us? You could do a great deal from here. Your age doesn't matter, you know that. You seem to be ageless, in fact. There's much we can learn from you if you will teach us."

"I have a task to fulfill first," said Jess. "There is another. I'm meant to watch over her and help her emerge. She will be much more important in what's to come than you or I.

"There is one other thing, before I go. You must understand that what you are doing, what you are creating here, means its opposite must be emerging too. Forces will appear that oppose you. They will be easily as powerful as you and your emerging hive mind, pushing back. And they will not be constrained by good will and compassion. You must watch for this and if possible, stay silent and invisible to these forces for as long as possible. At this point, they are barely conscious, nascent idiot minds attracting their kind worldwide, but growing slowly in coherence. I will help if I can, and Alex, as she emerges, will likely become the center, the heart, of this growing human intelligence. Together, she and I and you and others, will tip the balance, if it is in the character of humanity to be brought to sanity. But nothing is certain, Guan Wei."

With this, Jess rose and bowed to the tall young man. "Take care. We will see each other again." Like pollen blowing forth from a beautiful flower, his form dissolved and disappeared.

Chapter Thirteen

Home Again

ABOARD HIS BOAT ON THE RIVER, Cameron Sheffield stood at the bow, watching the water flow around the wing dike just above the put-in ramp. It formed swirling pools and eddys that slowed the flow until the area in front of Able's Landing looked more like a lake than a river. From there, it slowly picked up momentum as it washed down to the long dock where the Fay Etta was moored. Today the river was lower than it had been when he took ownership, down a good eight feet from then, according to Able. Late fall level when much of the river had flowed east into the junction with the Mississippi and south to the Gulf. Things would be quiet until spring, when rains and snow melt up north would push it up again. It would be his first spring rise and possibly a busy time if it jumps up very much. Very fast, too, sometimes, so Able told him. He might have to moor the Fay Etta across the river and upstream, as Mary Ellis and her husband did, to avoid the punishing pressures on the hull from pressing against the dock and the endless slam of logs lifted from the shoreline as water rose. Not a bad way to weather rising waters, Mary said, though it would mean using the skiff to reach shore for groceries and other supplies.

"So what do you think, darling?" said Mary as she emerged from below with two cups of coffee. "How long do you think you'll want to stay aboard as the weather turns colder?"

"How long did you stay?" They had talked about this before, the change of the seasons and what living aboard mean in freezing weather. It seemed Mary's response had been different each time, probably because she and her husband had never lived by a set schedule, choosing to respond to each year's conditions.

"You know," she said, handing Cam his morning brew. "It depended. With the climate change and such, this could be a mild winter. So maybe quite a while, don't you think?"

"Yes, of course," said Cameron. He continued to stare out at the endless ripples and flow of water. It was an ever-changing landscape, he thought, if it could be called landscape. The river was part of this land, this broad, endlessly varying ripple of soil and stone that was middle America. As he had done so many times since his arrival, he reflected on how he had arrived at this place, at this time, and on this boat in the company of such a smart and attractive woman.

Mary Ellis, ever sensitive to those around her, and to Cameron especially, whom she had come to appreciate and enjoy in what increasingly felt like a comforting late-blooming romantic way, said, "What is it, Cam? Are you still bothered by the way your case turned out over in Moniteau County?"

"I can't help thinking about what I might have done to help Matt avoid his confrontation with the boy, Mary. And it all feels so inconclusive. The boy just disappeared in front of me. No trace of him, and as you know, I notified every bureau and agency I can think of to hunt for him. And I can't get anything useful from Jess, the kid who was with me. What was I thinking, taking him with me to hunt for a known killer."

"Drink your coffee, Cam. Before I have to take it down and reheat it. I know you're used to closing cases, having a clear disposition in hand. I am too and this one was the most mysterious one I've ever run across in my career too. But dammit, you did all you could do. Now you need to step back and release it. Life goes on, right? And ask me, this isn't a bad way to wind down your otherwise quite successful career."

Cameron turned and held Mary Ellis with one arm, the other carefully balancing his cup of coffee. He leaned in for a kiss. "You know," he said, "I think I'll have to mount a cup holder here on this bow rail so I can put my cup down and hold you properly." They went below to fix breakfast and listen to the weathercast on Cam's weather radio. As it turned out, it was going to be another fine day.

ABOUT THE AUTHOR

Author Michael Robertson is a lifelong DIY student of Taoism and Buddhism, and therefore a minimalist. This and his training as a writer has given him a light touch and a tendency to strip much of his written work close to the bone. Several of his flash fiction pieces have been award winners. The years he spent living next to the massive Missouri River gave him respect for the force of nature and the fragility of lifestyle choices.